# NOT RUSSIAN

Mikhail Shevelev

# NOT RUSSIAN

*Translated from the Russian*
*by Brian James Baer and Ellen Vayner*

*With an Afterword*
*by Ludmila Ulitskaya*

Europa
*editions*

Europa Editions
27 Union Square West, Suite 302
New York, NY 10003
www.europaeditions.com
info@europaeditions.com

Copyright © Mikhail Shevelev, all rights reserved
Afterword © Ludmila Ulitskaya
Published by arrangement with ELKOST Intl. Literary Agency
First publication 2022 by Europa Editions

Translation by Brian James Baer and Ellen Vayner
Original title: Не русский
Translation copyright © 2022 by Europa Editions

Library of Congress Cataloging in Publication Data is available
ISBN 978-1-60945-811-9

Shevelev, Mikhail
Not Russian

Art direction by Emanuele Ragnisco
instagram.com/emanueleragnisco

Cover design by Ginevra Rapisardi

Cover photo: Shutterstock

Prepress by Grafica Punto Print – Rome

Printed in the USA

# CONTENTS

# NOT RUSSIAN

How many times have I told her: "Let's call someone to install another cable so we can put a TV in the kitchen." We end up spending most of our life there, but the TV's in the living room, so you have to either turn up the volume all the way or listen like a hunting dog to avoid missing something important. Obviously, it would be better to throw the television off the balcony considering what's on it, but don't we have to listen to the news? Aren't there shows that you watch from time to time? You say you watch TV to forget about things. And don't I need my soccer?

She tells me to go ahead and call someone. But when? I leave at eight in the morning and get back home at eight at night, if I'm lucky, or we'll have to spend the weekend waiting . . . he'll arrive sometime during the day. It's ridiculous. Okay, so we'll perk up our ears or blast the sound until our neighbors complain.

On that day we came home from work early, before the eight o'clock news. Tanya announces that she's a walking corpse who can only be brought back to life if served a cognac—here and now—no need to bother with snacks. After that drink, for once in her life, she drops down in front of the TV, leaving the honor of making dinner to me: "Fry some potatoes, make a salad, maybe pull out the cheese and salami, if you want—but I'll skip it. I've already put on almost two kilos since New Year's—don't forget the olives and throw a bottle of white wine in the freezer for a few minutes, today's a holiday after all . . . is that clear enough for you? And leave me alone for a while."

This, of course, was a domestic legend—about me making dinner once in a lifetime and her playing the prima donna. I make dinner as often as you do, my dear, don't give me that song and dance. And I don't mind it at all, quite the opposite—it's my simple way of showing you, dear, my love and affection. The fact that you don't even notice this act of domestic heroism done in honor of our relationship hurts deeply. I mean, it's a feat just finding the saltshaker! You, Tanya, are crazy; you always put everything in the wrong place . . . Oh, well, you'll have to eat the potatoes without salt . . . Tell me, what normal person puts a saltshaker *there*?

I heard the music from the opening of the *Vesti* evening news; that means it was already eight. "Turn it up! I'd like to listen to it too!"

At that moment my old pal Palych called. Following an unshakeable Soviet habit, he still watches the *Vremya* news at nine, so I guess he had the sudden urge to share some anecdote with me. To hell with the news, I decided. Tanya would tell me everything anyway, but I'd definitely forget to call Palych back, and he'd get upset. So, I closed the kitchen door, held the receiver against my shoulder, continued cutting vegetables for the salad and said: "Okay, let's hear your joke." It's a locker room joke, Palych warns me, but it's very funny. The locker room part was kind of obvious—what could you expect from a gynecologist—but the funny part . . . We'd have to see about that. "By the way, I sent a girl to your office the other day. When will you have her test results? Aha, I understand, but please, don't forget: I didn't send anyone to you, you've never seen me, and you don't even know who I am, but let's get back to your joke. No, I'm not having a relationship with that girl, she's the girlfriend of a friend, it's just to avoid any gossip . . ." The joke turned out to be long, truly from the locker room, and not funny, but I burst out laughing anyway, not to offend Palych.

I was standing with my back to the kitchen door and turned around even before Tanya screamed "Pasha!" A second before, I'd felt that something was wrong—she'd gotten up too suddenly—she was peacefully lying on the couch and then suddenly jumped up and swung the door open. "Palych, let me call you back," I said, realizing from the expression on her face that something terrible had happened. She was looking at me the way you look at a doctor who's just given you a fatal diagnosis—with fear, disgust, and deep pity for yourself.

The first thought that crossed my mind: "It's the end, I forgot to turn off my computer, she opened my email and found Sonya's messages, and this is really the end of everything because she'd never believe me, and honestly, who would?"

"There . . . they're asking for you . . ." she said in a voice that was hoarse, choked, alien. Tanya pointed in the direction of the living room, her hands shaking. Yeah, that must be it. Oh, shit! How could I be such a fool not to have checked my computer this morning. And that idiot with her emails . . . haven't we already said everything?! I walked into the living room with my head hung low.

The computer was off. The TV was on. I exhaled and asked what had happened. "Listen," she said. She wasn't talking but croaking. The phone rang in the kitchen. "Don't pick up, keep listening." "What's happened that's so bad? World War III?"

The news anchor was Ira Peregudina, a flashy brunette who was an intern at our newspaper during her sophomore year. And she's not stupid, not at all. It's unclear how she ended up in that zoo of ours, but, on the other hand, it's not so surprising. There are about two and a half decent newspapers left today, and even those are on the verge of bankruptcy. All this went through my mind after I'd recovered from the false alarm, but as soon as I realized what Ira was saying, I forgot about her, and about everything else.

"Unknown . . . The Church of the Epiphany in the village of Nikolskoye near Moscow . . . hostages . . . there are children . . . demands have not been announced . . . offered to send negotiators . . ." Oh, God! For so many years nothing like this had happened, not since Beslan . . . And then I heard my last name. And then another, which I also recognized.

Now both our phones, mine and Tanya's, were ringing nonstop. "Watch till the end," she said. From the TV: "At the time of the attack a video was posted on the Internet, in which one of the participants in the siege of the church talks about the upcoming operation . . ." A screenshot appeared on the TV: a blond guy about thirty years old. Well, now I understood how Zhenya and I were involved in all this. It was Vadik. This meant he hadn't died. He was alive.

Zhenya and I were able to get the last one released in September. It was Vadik. One Sergey and two Olegs were released before him, in May. But they didn't give us Vadik right away, so we had to go back.

Before that trip, Zhenya and I didn't really know each other; we just happened to eat at the same snack bar from time to time. Zhenya was a reporter at the network Vidy Sovremennosti, which rented an entire floor from my newspaper, *Moskovskii Kuryer*, in our building on Petrovka Street, which later became a hotel; and there was only one snack bar for all of us. At the time I was already an editor, with my own office, a secretary, and four subordinates. In addition to all those perks, I had another privilege, which I'd negotiated with the editor-in-chief, my pal Vitya Konev, when I agreed to exchange my carefree life as an observer to become an editor, and not just of any section, but of the section on ethnic conflicts. There was little fame in it, but I got three columns in every issue at a bare minimum. There was a lot going on in the ethnic conflicts section back then—as if Chechnya wasn't enough, there was the conflict between Abkhazia and South Ossetia, and then there was Transnistria, and Karabakh, and Tajikistan, and Muslims in the Ajaria region of Georgia, and some Russians practicing Judaism in the Voronezh province. Anyway, when our previous editor, Sasha Gureev, quit this loony bin overnight and went over to television, my answer to Konev's proposal was clear: "I'll only agree if you guarantee me at least one out-of-town assignment a month, otherwise, it's a no, because I'd drown in your ethnic minorities and go to hell as a journalist." He agreed.

And then, in the beginning of May, Yunusbek Yanbiev comes into my office and says: "I'm going to Nazran for the negotiations between the federal government and Maskhadov. It's unclear what the negotiations are all about, but you won't believe it, I've been included in the Russian delegation as an expert." "An expert in what field, may I ask? In bootleg vodka or forged invoices?" "Why do you care," Yunysbek says. "The most important thing is that I've been included; we'll figure the rest out later. And stop with your xenophobic comments, or I'll get upset and you'll lose this valuable source and be left reprinting old news reports from TASS . . . So, do you want to go to Nazran?"

Yunusbek was a real conman, and I wouldn't be surprised if he'd appointed himself an expert and a member of the delegation. He appeared at our newspaper a year before all this, when the war had just begun. He called up from the reception desk and announced: "I'm a Chechen, and I'm bringing you a plan for the peaceful resolution of the conflict." Back then the authors of such plans were overrunning the editorial offices of Moscow-based publications; they believed the craziness could easily be stopped if only as many people as possible were presented with the correct analysis, then everyone would come to their senses and the war would immediately come to an end. Moreover, as Yunusbek Yanbiev told us, he was the leader of the Chechen nationalist movement Sun of the World. I gave in: "Okay, let's talk." You never know in advance with these self-appointed saviors—most of the time, they're your average nutjob, but every once in a while they give you something useful.

Obviously, Yunusbek had coined the name Sun of the World to lend himself an air of importance—the entire organization consisted of a single member, him. But the guy turned out to be smart, sincere, although not without ambition, and useful—that was the main thing. Yunusbek was a Chechen born in Moscow but with vast family ties; he often visited his homeland and knew what was happening there; he could make sense of the local clans, or *teips,* and their tangled relationships, but most importantly, he could explain all of it in comprehensible Russian. Yunusbek's ambitions were of a political nature: he hoped one day to become nothing less than the president of Chechnya. And why not, if Dudayev could do it? He needed me because, as any idiot knew, it's impossible to achieve anything in politics without media support.

The idea of going to Nazran was very tempting. Negotiations were taking place between the government and Maskhadov—if we were lucky, and Yunusbek with his Chechen connections had really dug up something interesting, we'd get a full-page story. And if we weren't lucky, there'd be enough material for a column. Plus, it was time for me to get out of the office. You spend days on end editing all kinds of crap, not writing anything yourself, letting your talent go to waste—and suddenly you're no longer a hero among the secretaries; you've been replaced by someone from the reference department. And this week Tanya would be taking care of her child who was on break from school, so I wouldn't be able to see her on the weekend anyway. It would take one day to get to Nazran, we'd spend two-three days there, and then back; making it into the next issue should be doable.

Of course, the editor-in-chief immediately rejected the idea: "Who'd be left to work if I let everyone go on assignment." That was only to be expected—he had to point out that he was doing me a huge favor and that I'd owe him one. After haggling for a while, we decided that I'd go to Nazran, but only for three days, including travel. Okay, so be it, but if I need to, I'll just say there weren't any return tickets—he can check for himself. As I was leaving Vitya's office, he suddenly remembered something: "Hey, there's one more thing—I made an agreement with Sasha Nelyubin from *Vidy Sovremennosti* to let their journalists come along on our assignments—they are totally clueless, and the stories they bring back are enough to make their editors jump out the window. And in return for our intellectual help, they'll advertise us on TV, something like, 'This story was prepared with the invaluable support of the newspaper *Moskovsky Kuryer*.' Stop by their office on the third floor and tell them about your idea. Maybe they'll be interested."

Picking your traveling companion for an assignment—that's a delicate matter; you can't force it. When you work in a pair, it's usually a reporter and a cameraman, and it takes a long time for you to form a team. No one likes strangers in our business; you never know who you might end up with—a drunk, a bore, a coward, or just an idiot. In Moscow you can easily get rid of them, but it's not an option on an out-of-town assignment—you have to put up with them until the end, when you land at Sheremetyevo, Domodedovo, or Vnukovo. Only then can you tell them everything that was building up inside you over the course of the trip, then listen to what they have to say in return, and possibly end up in a fist fight. It's happened before.

Well, our newspaper could use some TV advertising, especially on a program like *Oko*, which was aired on Vidy Sovremennosti; no one could argue with that. And so, I went to the Vidy Sovremennosti offices on the third floor, during their staff meeting, and told them: "Konev sent me to tell you about Nazran, the negotiations, about Stepashin and Mikhailov from the government and Maskhadov from the other side. We have a source. I'm going. Are you interested?"

Our staff meetings are like a popular assembly, where everyone can express their opinion on every topic, but at *Oko*, there was unity of command. Nelyubin and Kushner made the decisions, the others listened. Kushner says: "Styopin, pack your bags." And a guy who looks vaguely familiar stands up. Zhenya Styopin was a big guy, about five years younger than me and two heads taller. I say: "Let's go, partner. We need to decide who's bringing what and where. Have you ever worked in the Caucasus?"

He had worked in the Caucasus. While filming some monasteries in Karabakh, he had a chance to visit Chechnya, so he was offended by my question, and the whole next day, as we drove to the airport, flew to Narzan and then made our way to the Assa Hotel, the only decent one in town, he barely spoke to me, and only out of absolute necessity. That evening, in the hotel room, after we'd had something to eat and drink, he finally got over it, and we started talking.

Zhenya turned out to be quite a character. He'd worked at a local TV station in Voronezh, then decided to try his luck in Moscow. He just up and left, eventually finding his way to *Oko*. He was without house or home, he rented different apartments . . . and had a wife and a two-year-old child. It was a nomadic existence, but then half our staff lived that way, unsettled. He was charming, artistic, well-read, an excellent storyteller, and he knew how to listen—a very uncommon skill for someone working in TV. However, being a nice guy is not a profession; tomorrow we'd see how good he was at his job.

But Zhenya didn't get a chance to prove his professionalism, not the next day or the two days after that.

The negotiations had begun and were ongoing. Stepashin arrived, then Maskhadov showed up. That evening, they left. And that's it, nothing, literally nothing else was happening. I could still find something to do—I walked around the burning-hot courtyard of the Ingush parliament, where the negotiations were taking place, collected gossip, and exchanged anecdotes with Maria Eismont from *Segodnya* and Mark Deitch of *Moskovsky Komsomolets*. From time to time, I tried to catch Yunusbek, who turned out to be an actual member of the delegation, but following this sudden career leap, he'd become very important and secretive.

For Zhenya, this was a catastrophe. He needed visuals and action: "It's television, you know, not a newspaper!" But for three days, it was like a cemetery in a desert. It took him only half a day to shoot some footage of Nazran, the arrival of the Russian delegation, and Maskhadov's picturesque security detail. The rest was creative downtime, which was accompanied by depression. He complained that if he returned empty-handed, he'd be demoted to a production editor and sent to the cutting room for two months. In addition to the shame, it would be a financial catastrophe. Besides creative satisfaction and recognition, out-of-town assignments usually brought a notice-able bump in salary because no accountant would ever request receipts from someone who'd just returned from a war zone. You bring them your plane tickets, and that's it; how you spend the rest of the money is no one's business. "It's been a long time since I've had any per diem money"—any intern in any newspa-per knows what this phrase means. Depressed by his impending doom, Zhenya even refused to drink with us at night.

But what could I do? Negotiations are not like the freeing of the Budyenovsk hostages from Basayev's separatists; with nego-tiations, you need to think. So, I told him to go and film rebel fighters peacefully conversing with the federal negotiators. Or, if he liked, I could bring him some Ingush leader. Or, he could always film a mosque at sunset and use it later for cutaways.

No, all this wasn't good enough. Zhenya needed a western, a gun fight—it didn't matter who was shooting whom—as long as there was a lot of blood and a flag flying over ruins seized by unknown forces . . . basically, he needed some action.

On the third day of waiting in front of the doors of the Ingush parliament, he got some action.

Yunusbek appeared on the steps, looked for me in the

crowd, and nodded in the direction of the street. We met outside the gates. It was written all over his face: he had news, and it was very important.

"Why have you been avoiding me for the last three days?"

"They ordered us not to talk to the press. If they saw us talking to a journalist, they wouldn't let us back into the negotiations. But that's not important. Listen to me, they've reached an agreement, the government negotiators and Maskhadov. Chernomyrdin called Stepashin and told him to stop stalling. He had to deliver results to Yeltsin, but the government negotiators had been sitting with their thumbs up their asses for days. They were on speaker, so I could hear them from the hallway."

"What did they agree to?"

"There will be a cease-fire, then—new negotiations. And after that, there'll be peace, I guess."

"No way!"

"Go! They'll be announcing it any minute now. There won't be a press conference; they'll just make a statement and leave. Maskhadov will give a press conference the day after tomorrow in the village of Starye-Atagi. There's more. I have a relative, Lechi Sultygov, in Maskhadov's security detail. He can take you in his car and try to arrange for you to have a special interview with Maskhsdov during the trip."

"What about you?"

"I'll go with them too."

"But you're a member of the Russian delegation."

"I was, until today. The negations are over, which means the delegations don't exist anymore. I'm free. Now I want to smooth things over with Maskhadov's crew—it'd be a bonus for me."

If only Yunusbek knew the kind of trouble he was getting into by "smoothing things over." But that would become clear only later.

In the meantime, I ran to find Zhenya to tell him about the

truce and about us potentially getting an exclusive, which would make us heroes, legendary figures of Russian journalism, and so he could stop lamenting the loss of his side-income.

I found Zhenya already in the hall where the negotiations had been taking place. Using his size to his advantage and ignoring the protests of his colleagues, he'd fought his way to the front row and was mounting his camera on a tripod.

"Where the hell were you?" he asks. "They're saying the truce will be announced any minute now."

"Yes, it's true. Yunusbek gave me a heads-up. But, listen, there's more."

At that moment Stepashin and Maskhadov entered the hall and confirmed what everyone had been discussing for the last fifteen minutes. All the reporters for the major agencies had long ago run to the phones to pass on the sensational news—to Moscow, London, and New York. "The war is over," Maskhadov said before leaving and, with his signature gesture, he struck his open palm with his fist, as if sealing the deal. Well, that remained to be seen . . .

After we'd made our way outside along with the excited crowd, I explained our plan of action to Zhenya. First, we'd run to the hotel, grab our stuff, check out, and then spend the night with Maskhadov's security detail—Yunusbek had already arranged it. In the morning, we'd travel an unknown path, at the end of which lay fame and fortune. But before that, I needed to get to a phone to dictate a story about this historic event—no more than five thousand characters, just to make it into this issue—then reserve an entire page for the next one. Then I'd call my parents and Tanya so they wouldn't be worried, and we could be on our way.

The men guarding the commander of the Chechen separatists had a resolute look; they were covered in firearms from head to toe. But they were friendly with us. First of all, Yunusbek hadn't lied about his family connections. Second of all, when we were asked the test question "Are you for peace?" we answered in the affirmative. What fool would be against peace in such company? *Moskovsky Kuryer* made no impression on the bodyguards, but they thought the program *Oko*, which was broadcast on Channel One, was legit. On that day, with his camera and tripod, which the bodyguards carried for him out of respect, Zhenya became an equal partner, if not the leader, in our collaboration.

The first night lived up to our most optimistic expectations. We stayed on the outskirts of Nazran in a red-brick house, a symbol of prosperity for the Vainakh people, in a room with rug-covered walls and sectional furniture from Yugoslavia— Soviet chic. Around three o'clock in the morning, Zhenya got up to take a piss and accidently knocked over a machine gun that had been leaning against the wall near the door; it landed on his foot. The weapon turned out to be heavy. Zhenya swore in two languages but went back to sleep completely happy. It was now clear that our creative downtime was over and that the real action had begun.

That morning we left Nazran and headed to Chechnya. We didn't take the main highway, the Bakinka, but traveled along winding country roads through Urus-Martan and a bunch of villages that were indistinguishable from one another. This was a triumphal march. The green, white, and red flags of Ichkeria were hanging from the windows of our SUVs and trucks, the locals—women, children, and the elderly—were laying rugs under the wheels of our vehicles and greeting us with flatbread and Fanta. The Chechen hit song of that spring was playing at full blast: "Dzhokhar will never die!" It was over, there was a truce—so we hadn't fought and died for nothing. Yeltsin— that asshole, that bastard, that son of a bitch—had finally stopped. Even when two land mines exploded on our way to Grozny, no one paid much attention—another provocation, oh well, what else could you expect. The main thing was that the truce was signed. Zhenya was shooting footage almost non-stop, leaning his entire upper body out the truck window.

We reached Starye-Atagi toward evening. We learned that somewhere along the way our column had split into two. Maskhadov had gone to the mountains, and the location of his press conference had been changed. It would take place tomorrow, not here but in the town of Makhkety.

The next morning, we were loaded onto a Ural truck, clearly a war trophy, that drove us straight up a rocky mountain river. Despite the truce, there were still plenty of checkpoints on the roads, and it was unclear whether the guys manning them had even heard the war was over. Plus, every other person in our convoy was on the federal government's most wanted list—some for Budyonovsk, some for Pervomayskoye, and some for Bamut. So, the river road was a safer bet.

By the time we made it to Makhkety, the usual media crowd was already there, having migrated from Nazran. "What's new" was our first question. We had no TV, no newspapers. Nothing really had happened . . . Spartak lost, the dollar rose . . . Somewhere in Europe, Yeltsin had given a speech: "The constitutional order in Chechnya has, on the whole, been restored, and now, well, by joint effort we will try to restore normal life, you understand . . ." Was he at least sober? It was hard to tell anymore.

Maskhadov didn't show up at the press conference. Yandarbiyev Movladi Udurov appeared in his place. The former became president after Dudayev was hit by a rocket six months ago, while the latter was the leading Chechen spokesperson and ideologue. The conference was organized in a private residence. I had never before seen a press conference where everyone, from the journalists to the speakers, took their shoes off at the door, as is the custom in a Muslim home, and asked and answered questions in their stocking feet. Yandarbayev tried hard to look important, but Udugov did most of the talking. He was the one who announced, while wriggling his toes, that a major step had been taken in negotiating a cease-fire.

Okay, this was all great, and we, as unwavering supporters of peace, were insanely happy, but where was Maskhadov, our promised exclusive? And where had Yunusbek gotten off to?

As to the question about Yunusbek's whereabouts, we received a very evasive answer from his relative Lechi Sultygov, a stocky forty-something and an exemplary specimen of a charming bandit. As for Maskhadov, this was the situation: "You'll go to my place, settle in, have dinner, and wait for him. He'll come when he comes. He has many things to do besides your interview."

Maskhadov never showed up. Instead, Lechi offered us Basayev, who was ready to talk to us tomorrow night. Would that work? We got upset. It was almost a year since Budyonovsk, and *Pionerskaya Pravda* was probably the only media outlet that hadn't published something on Basayev. Moreover, Yelena Masyuk from *NTV*, who was the first to nab an interview with him, had already skimmed the cream off the top. But Maskhadov had kept silent this whole time, not giving a single interview, not to anyone. And the most annoying thing was that I'd already promised him for the next issue. I knew what I'd hear back in Moscow: "You've been hanging around all this time, promising Maskhadov, and instead you bring us this garbage . . ." And if Basayev might do in a pinch for *Moskovsky Kuryer*, an interview with a leading Chechen terrorist would be a total no-go for national TV, especially for Channel One.

On the other hand, Basayev was better than nothing. Plus, truth be told, I was curious to see him in person—people like that don't come around every day.

Before that, I'd seen him just once, in September of 1991, in Grozny, when the Soviet government was driven out and the office of the former first secretary of the Party was occupied by the leader of the rebellion, the Soviet general Dudayev, dressed in combat fatigues and a cap. Reaching the North Pole would have been easier for him than grasping what was going on and what he'd gotten himself into. And in the reception area, where a secretary was promising over the phone to put someone in front of a firing squad in the name of the Chechen revolution, there in the corner sat a quiet, balding young man with a beard. Only his eyes stood out. The young man had the gaze of a German Shepherd before it attacks—intent but indifferent. Someone told me it was Shamil Basayev, who had just returned from a Turkish prison where he'd been sentenced for hijacking a plane from Mineralnye Vody to Ankara a month before. Who'd have thought that was only the beginning of his career?

"Okay, we'll take Basayev," I said. Zhenya and I were annoyed, but even a mangy sheep is good for a little wool.

He showed up the next evening. Two cars pulled up carrying five bodyguards who made the guys in Maskhadov's security detail look like Prussians soldiers; these were real criminals. Then came a third car, from which Basayev emerged. He was completely bald now, but his beard was even thicker. "Hello, why don't we have dinner first, then relax a bit, and have the interview in the evening?" "Okay." We sat down for dinner, looking one another over and talking about nothing, and then—a cultural interlude. We watched the film *Braveheart*, about the heroic struggle of Scottish separatists against English colonizers. Not surprisingly, it was the most popular film in Chechnya and Ingushetia. We'd already watched it twice at our hotel in Nazran, but it would have been dumb to refuse.

With the video at full volume and the spectators cheering the Scots at the top of their lungs, I whispered into Zhenya's ear: "Do you want to become a Hero of the Russian Federation?" I pointed with my eyes to the weapons piled up in the corner of the room. I then straightened my head and met Basayev's gaze.

"I wouldn't recommend it," he said cheerfully. How could he have heard anything in that noise? A real German Shepherd, as I said.

At nightfall, when everyone had settled down, Zhenya mounted his camera, set up some lighting with whatever was at hand, and we began talking. I decided not to ask Basayev about Budyenovsk or about the war in general. He'd already talked about it hundreds of times and it would be impossible to get anything new. "So, let's talk about your childhood and adolescence, and especially about you as a young man. What made you into the Basayev you are today? You haven't been fighting all your life, have you?"

Suddenly Basayev started talking, and he seemed to enjoy reminiscing.

He came to Moscow in 1985, tried twice to get into law school at Moscow State University, but was unsuccessful both times. His friends kept telling him that he'd need to bribe someone, but he refused to believe it. He lived with friends in their dorm rooms and began working as a night watchman at a little hole-in-the-wall restaurant in the Paveletsky train station, then as a controller at the city tram and trolleybus depot, where everyone was stealing coins from the registers after their shifts, but that was beneath him. Finally, he got accepted into a university—not Moscow State law school but an institute for future land surveyors. He had finished his first two years when Gorbachev's Law on Cooperatives came into effect. You could now buy and sell things—anything was possible. And so, it began. You'd sell computers here and buy jeans there, then put the profits back into your business: there were sit-downs and shoot-outs, your first set of wheels, living the good life. Back then, everyone was getting rich the same way. This free-for-all lasted until September 1991, when Dudayev seized power in Chechnya and proclaimed its independence, without realizing what that actually meant. Moscow threatened to send in troops. This is when Basayev sold almost everything off quickly and left for Grozny. He never returned to Moscow.

His first major act was hijacking the plane from Mineralnye Vody to Turkey—that's how he responded to the threat of sending in troops. He fell out with Dudayev pretty quickly, and Basayev began wandering with his militia throughout the Caucasus region. He fought in Karabakh on the Azeri side, but he wasn't happy with the Azeris—cowardly, boneheaded sheep. He moved to Abkhazia to fight with the Georgians and worked his way up to vice-minister of defense. Then the war in Chechnya broke out and he, naturally, returned. Then his relatives were killed in bombing raids—seventeen, including children. And after that, there was Budyonovsk. He got interested in Islam while living in Moscow, but it was only during the war that he read the entire Koran. "A Jewish plot against Muslims? Only fools believe in conspiracies. The Russian people? They're the same as every other nation, but the Russians are so downtrodden, you can really have your way with them . . ."

Was Basayev lying? He didn't seem to be. And what would be the point? He'd already done enough to earn himself the death penalty, regardless of anything he had to say about his difficult youth and the Russian people. Basayev wasn't trying to justify his actions. Maybe he wasn't being totally honest about the Koran—I don't think he read it; most likely Udugov summarized it for him.

"Okay, it's a take. Let's wrap it up, Zhenya."

When we got up the next morning, there was no trace of Basayev and his fellow film buffs. Lechi explained that he never stayed in one place longer than a day and that he always left before sunrise. A smart strategy for someone with his history.

We had to get going too; we'd gotten everything we could out of this place. Zhenya asked for forty more minutes. He needed some footage of Maskhedy—he'd find a small hill, shoot fast, and we'd leave. "Okay, go, and I'll try to find our lost Yunusbek. Lechi, where can I find your relative, the former member of the Russian delegation?" Lechi was visibly unhappy with my questions about Yunusbek, but he didn't lie—he didn't know where he was.

Lechi explained: "The local people have questions for Yunusbek: Who is he, where's he from, why is he here? They don't have any questions for you, but Yunusbek is a different story. He's a Chechen, and in Nazran he was with the Russians, everybody saw it, and it looked suspicious. Personally, I believe him, but let the people talk to him and put their minds at ease."

"No, that's not going to happen. We came together, he's our friend, so you'll have to arrange for us to see him. I want to make sure that you're not holding him in the local *zindan*, and that you haven't cut him into pieces." Lechi smiled and led me to the next street, where we found Yunusbek in one of the houses. He was alive, still in one piece, but in a foul mood. "Have you had any problem making contact with Maskhedov's people?" I asked. "Can I help with anything?"

"I don't need anything. They're just obsessed with spies and so they've been keeping me here for three days, asking all sorts of idiotic questions. And now they've sent someone to the village I come from—to check if I'm telling the truth. Ichkerian peasants!"

"Okay, then, I'll see you back in Moscow."

I returned to our place and found Zhenya in a highly agitated state. "What happened?" While searching for the perfect vantage point for his footage, he'd walked down a narrow path behind Lechi's house and ran into four guys digging a ditch. Russians. "Who are you, what are doing here?" Zhenya asked. It turned out they were prisoners of war. First, they'd been held in the village of Shatoy, then they were sold here, in

Makhkety. "Life's not so bad here, it's okay. Of course, they make us work, but they feed us too; they don't beat us or torture us. There's a heater in the barn where they keep us." They didn't attempt to run away—they saw what had happened to those who tried; they wouldn't be executed, but nothing good would come of it.

Sergey and two Olegs were taken prisoner near the town of Shali. Their infantry fighting vehicle had broken down and they were left to guard it. They got inside it at night to escape the cold. Another vehicle approached, and someone knocked on the armor: "Get out, or we'll throw a grenade." Vadik, the fourth prisoner, was captured in a different location. Since then, they had little idea of what was going on outside their barn, let alone outside Mashkety, and of what fate had in store for them.

At this moment, Zhenya came up with a noble but totally crazy idea: "Should we try to rescue them?"

"But how? Who would release them to us?"

As strange as it may seem, we found an unexpectedly easy solution to the problem of freeing the soldiers. Lechi proposed an exchange: "Film me and give me your word that it'll be aired on the program *Oko*, and I'll release the prisoners."

"Will you air the footage?" I asked Zhenya. "No problem. Four rescued prisoners of war—that isn't just a program, that's more of a heroic feat, something like: The program *Oko* brings our guys back home." Nelyubin and Kushner will die from jealousy, but they won't pass up the opportunity. "This will earn us a TAFI award, I guarantee it." "But how will we get them to Moscow? It won't be that hard to get through the Chechen checkpoints, we know the price, a bottle of vodka per vehicle, but then what? How would we get on a plane? They don't have passports or any of the other documents you need to buy tickets. We can go by train, but the first station patrol will arrest them, and us in the bargain. Only we think of them as prisoners of war, you know; for the authorities—they're deserters."

At this point, Lechi, the owner of the goods in question, entered the conversation: "Take them to Makhachkala," he said. "Nadir Khachilayev is there; he'll help. I know for a fact that he helps prisoners of war. His brother Mahomed is the minister of fisheries, and if you need it, Nadir can even get you to America from Makhachkala."

As we spoke, the idea began to seem less crazy.

Zhenya quickly mounted his camera on the tripod and set up a backdrop. With the rescued prisoners in the background, Lechi read the inspiring script about the war that I'd written for him. Then he ad-libbed a finale—a machine gun burst into the air. "Idiot," Zhenya said. "Why are you shooting right in front of the camera? It messed up the sound." After a statement like that, I thought we'd be executed on the spot along with the other poor bastards. But nothing of the kind happened: Lechi looked down sheepishly and obediently went to record the second take. You can say what you want about television, but as I'm constantly reminded, it's more powerful than newspapers.

There was only one problem we couldn't solve. Lechi agreed to free all four guys but not at once—in two stages. "You can take three of them now and then come back later for the last one," Lechi said. "The ditch has to be finished even under the new conditions of the truce—that's reason number one. Besides, the six of you would never fit in one car, especially with Zhenya's equipment and given his size." So, it was decided that we'd take Sergey and the two Olegs and leave Vadik in Makhkety, as he was the biggest of the four—even for five of us it was going to be very crowded inside the Zhiguli. "Don't worry," we reassured Vadik. "We'll definitely come back for you."

"When will the story air?" Lechi asked. "Friday, 9 P.M., you can watch it, of course, as long as we don't get arrested." As we said our goodbyes, we hugged in the Chechen way—barely touching shoulders. Lechi turned out to be a great guy, even though he'd let them arrest our Yunusbek for no apparent reason, and he was holding Vadik not so much to dig the ditch but as insurance—so we didn't get the idea of tricking him and not broadcasting his appeal to the peoples of Russia.

We passed seventeen checkpoints on our way from Makhkety to Makhachkala, buying vodka—the price of safe passage—in local markets along the way. We reached the house of Nadir Khachilayev toward evening. In the city, we asked passersby for directions, and everyone knew exactly where this mysterious philanthropist lived.

An entrance guarded by marble lions, a wrought-iron gate, and a three-meter-high brick wall—it's not bad being the brother of the minister of fisheries. It was clear that if a serious guy like the owner of this house wasn't able to help us, then we were in real trouble, and our adventure had reached a dead end. The security staff heard us out, went inside to report, and then came back with the message: "Nadir isn't home, but we reached him by phone. He'll be back in about two hours, and then we can sort everything out. But for now, please come in and have dinner." This meant we'd been accorded the status of guest—which was already a step in the right direction.

The most memorable thing in Nadir Khachilayev's house was a collection of Kalashnikovs hanging on the living room wall—the machine guns were of every possible variety, each with its own story. We were served black caviar. The master of the house—whose manner of conducting himself was surprisingly like that of Shamil Basayev—showed up late that night. "So, tell us again who you are and what you need. *Oko, Moskovsky Kuryer*? How many prisoners did you say? And they don't have any identification papers? I see. Magomed, call and find out when the first flight to Moscow is tomorrow. Go to sleep now, we'll take off at eight tomorrow morning and get you out of here. Don't worry."

The secret behind this hospitality was simple. For some reason, our host refused to be filmed for our piece on the release of the prisoners of war, but he did ask that we add a credit informing the TV audience that the program *Oko* was very grateful to Nadir Khachilayev, the leader of the Lak people, for his help and support.

The next day we saw why the leader of the Lak people was so confident we'd be able to leave Makhachkala without any problems. That morning a motorcade appeared in the courtyard. It consisted of two Hummers and a white G-class Mercedes-Benz with the master of the house behind the wheel. The approximately ten guys in his entourage stood out from ordinary bystanders by the Stechkin automatic pistols defiantly holstered under their belts. Khachilayev negotiated with the manager of the airport without leaving his car, and the negotiations didn't last long. As soon as they were over, our motorcade drove straight to the runway, and we boarded the flight to Moscow like a typical government delegation. The guys accompanying us laughed when we offered to pay for our tickets.

The day before, we'd been able to reach the parents of the one Sergey and the two Olegs by phone, and they managed to get to Moscow from Kineshma, Vladimir, and a village near Astrakhan. We transferred our precious cargo to them right there, in Vnukovo airport, and they gave us whatever they had time to grab from their refrigerators: a jar of marinated mushrooms, a pound of lard, a three-liter bottle of *samogon*. "Don't worry, it's pure, made from sugar." "Thank you!" "No, thank *you*!" The former prisoners of war rushed to their parents without even saying goodbye. "I get it," I remarked. "Can you imagine what was going on in their heads? The day before yesterday, they were digging a ditch in Makhkety, then there was the road where every checkpoint made them tremble, then Nadir with his Hummers. And that was probably the first time they ever saw the inside of an airplane."

"There's a lot going on in my head, too," Zhenya answered. "I'd rather be home in bed, with my wife, but I'll go to Ostankino and put the piece together, otherwise it won't make it into the next show. Lechi's already told the whole village he'll be on TV. He'll be so disappointed if he doesn't see himself on the air, he'll bury Vadik in that ditch."

"Okay, see you later. I'm off."

"When are we going back for Vadik? We promised."

"Right, we'll talk."

Moscow's not a city, it's a total swamp that sucks you in the moment you enter. First, it's one thing, then another, then a whole list of things. First, I'm in charge of the next issue, then Zhenya's being sent to Kemerovo to film some coal miners, then Tanya's getting clingy: "No, don't go, I can't take it anymore, I miss you." Then my mother has another heart attack . . . In short, we didn't go back for Vadik until September.

But things were totally different now. The truce hadn't even lasted for two months. In Moscow someone snapped, and on TV it was the usual broken record about stamping out the monster of separatism and keeping Russia united. And so, a vicious circle began to spin: shootings and bombings returned, columns of tanks went into gorges where, as usual, the tanks were set on fire. Then, in the air space right above the Khankala military base, an Mi-8 helicopter full of police generals was shot down, and, in return, they started to round up all the men over eighteen in the nearby villages. And then we show up, like two massive idiots, on our humanitarian mission to rescue the soldier, Vadik. Wise people had told us: Go now, who the hell knows what might happen later. Well, alright. There's no getting out of it. We'll have to think of something.

This is what we came up with: We'd get travel documents

for a Vidy Sovremennosti cameraman Vadim Petrovich Seryogin—that's Vadik's full name—with all the necessary stamps and seals, then we'd bring some decent civilian clothes with us in Vadik's size and, with brazen self-confidence, we'd get him onto a plane bound for Moscow, while telling anyone who might ask the tragic story of our cameraman who had lost his documents.

In Makhkety, we were welcomed like family. Zhenya barely made any cuts to the story with Lechi, and now he'd become the most recognizable person in the village, and not only in his village—relatives from Vedeno came to spend some time with the celebrity. And so, we got Vadik released without a hitch and started on our way back.

To play it safe, we decided not to fly out of the Grozny air-port where there were more security guards than passengers; instead, we took the familiar route, through Makhachkala, where Nadir lived. We weren't too eager to see him again, but he could be useful as a back-up in case something went wrong. Luckily, we didn't need Nadir in the end.

Our plan worked out, even though every obstacle put us on the brink of failure and scandal, as we learned when we got back to Moscow.

After we reached Makhachkala and successfully sold our story to the airport ticket office about the cameraman Seryogin who'd lost his documents, we got tickets for the first available flight, which was in two days, and then began a drinking marathon at a nearby hotel. Claiming humanitarian reasons as the purpose of our trip, we'd asked for travel papers for one week and received the per diem for one week too—so we had plenty of money. "Heavy drinking while waiting for a flight invariably leads to a weakening of vigilance"—this is what Dima Strelkov from the information section wrote in his explana-tory letter after it came to light that he'd written his brilliant story on the fight against narcotraffic in Tadzhikistan, which was filled with sparkling details, while sitting in a restaurant in Sheremetyevo airport, where he spent two days, which was as long as his per diem allowed. A similar weakening of vigilance happened with us when it became clear that everything was going well and that nothing could stop us.

About three hours before our flight, Zhenya said he had to go to the local market to buy some black caviar for his kid. I tried to reason with him, but it was a lost cause—he rarely experienced parental emotions, but when he did, they were hard to extinguish.

The caviar was, of course, confiscated at the airport, luckily, without criminal charges. But only when we arrived at my place on the outskirts of Moscow and sat around the table did we learn just how close we'd been to failure. "Wait a second," Vadik said, "I have a gift for you." We shrugged our shoulders. He hadn't been out of our presence for a second, so he must have gone somewhere in the airport to buy us a bottle as a thank you gift? But where did he get the money?

"Did you give him any money?"

"No, I didn't have anything left."

"Well, okay, let's wait and see."

Vadik came back to the kitchen holding a small package of roughly two hundred grams.

"This is really good weed," he said. "I knew you didn't lie and that you'd come back for me, so I was saving it. I barely touched it. But be careful, this weed is really strong."

"But how did you manage to get it through security?"

"I tied it to my leg."

"Excellent! Now, Zhenya, remember what I told you back in Makhachkala and just imagine that we were arrested because of your caviar and taken to jail, where they'd find weed on Vadik, at which point it becomes clear that he was no cameraman. And so, we're sitting in the local precinct when our colleagues back in Moscow are reading the police report:

We would like to bring to your attention . . . using false documents . . . under the pretense of rescuing prisoners of
war . . . one kilogram of black-market caviar and two hundred
grams of an illegal plant-based drug . . . a case has been opened
in accordance with Article . . ."

"Yeah," Zhenya said, "You, Vadik, are an asshole, and I'm
no better. On the other hand, what can we do about it now?
Are you suggesting we don't smoke it?"

Vadik lived with me for a while, then moved into Zhenya's
rental apartment. Later, in our building on Petrovka Street, we
found a small storage closet that no one used and that everyone had forgotten about. We made a deal with the building
manager, broke the lock, brought in a mattress and some kind
of dresser, and Vadik moved in.

He adamantly refused to return to his hometown of
Novomoskovsk. Even his mother had no idea who his father
was, plus she was no prize—when Vadik was seven years old,
she dumped him on her cousin and became a popular enter-
tainer in the local dive bars. And she wasn't exactly famous for
her singing . . .

While Vadik was in Chechnya, his aunt got married and left,
as rumor had it, for Arkhangelsk, without leaving more precise
coordinates. We learned all this after Zhenya and I insisted that
Vadik visit his hometown at least once. "Are you going to keep
living without a passport? With only your documents from your
business trip? Have you by any chance forgotten they're fake?"
Right around that time the government granted amnesty to
people like Vadik, who'd been harmed in the process of
rebuilding the constitutional order in the Northern Caucasus.
But to be on the safe side, we asked Slava Izmeilov from *Novaya
Gazeta* to call the military enlistment office in Novomoskovsk
and ask them for a favor. So, no one asked Vadik any questions.
After a week, he returned with a passport and the news about
his lost aunt and, consequently, the loss of a place to live.

"Did you find your mom?"

"I didn't even look for her."

Since there was now a place for Vadik to live in Moscow, the only question remaining was—on what income. But this was easily resolved: there were jobs loading and unloading freight at railroad stations or jobs at construction sites, where no one asks about anything, jobs putting up posters or washing cars. In Moscow, which was getting richer by the hour, there were plenty of random jobs on every corner. And when he was suddenly short on cash, he'd borrow some from me or Zhenya, always paying us back on time, despite our protestations. Such earnings were more than enough for Vadik's shopping at the Cherkizovsky market. He didn't have to worry about food. The girls from accounting would feed him during the day, and for dinner he was usually invited to the proofing department where they always worked late, or he would eat with the drivers.

The only time he spent in his closet was at night; when he wasn't working, he'd spend all his free time in my office or in Zhenya's editing room. Everyone at the newspaper got used to Vadik and didn't just try to help him, they were proud of him, the way people are proud of a valuable trophy—in the sense that he was a living symbol of the effectiveness of our media outlets. The war was already over, and Vadik symbolized our contribution to the cause of peace. Plus, he happened to be a good guy, always eager to lend a hand, to go and get beer or cigarettes or to help carry heavy stuff. The only thing was—he was too quiet. Neither Vadik nor anyone else had really thought about what would happen to him in the future. From time to time a newly appointed manager tried to kick Vadik out of his dwelling, but in response, without fail, the women at the newspaper would gather, then head off to give the manager a tongue-lashing, after which everything would go back to normal and life would continue on in its usual way. This lasted for about two years, maybe a bit longer.

The situation changed in 1998, with the economic crisis. On August 14, Yeltsin gave a speech assuring people that everything would be fine with the Russian ruble, but on August 18 it collapsed—then came default and depreciation. Anyone who didn't know what that meant learned fast: salaries dropped by two to three times while prices went in the opposite direction. Devastation and catastrophe everywhere, everything was closing, and people were losing their jobs in droves.

Soon it reached us too. Circulation was declining and advertisers were disappearing; no one was issuing loans. It became clear that the building on Petrovka Street was an unaffordable luxury for *Moskovsky Kuryer*. The building would have to be sold, and we would need to move out—but try to find a buyer. All renters were let go, although by then we had only one left, Vidy Sovremennosti. We sold the building, moved out, found a new place in the business center near Danilovsky Market, right across from the psychiatric hospital. At this point, it became clear that there was no room for Vadik at our new offices. No room at all. Our building on Petrovka Street was built before the Revolution and had a storage closet, but here—there was one large open space for the journalists, two offices with glass walls, mine and Tanya's, and a meeting room. So where could we put Vadik?

Zhenya and I tried to help, looking for different solutions—maybe someone needs a house sitter for their *dacha*, or for who knows what—but it was all in vain. After the crisis, anyone who wasn't bankrupt yet would default tomorrow, and all of yesterday's moneybags and big spenders were turning into semi-destitute hoarders right before our eyes. It also became very difficult to make any money; there were a lot of people like Vadik—hardworking, but without skills. Crowds of Vadik-like people were roaming the city in the search of income, but all the employers were fleeing. So, Vadik found his own solution: he got married.

Where he picked her up, or she picked him up, we didn't even ask. She was a typical girl from the outskirts of Moscow, a bottle brunette with a half-kilo of cheap makeup on her face. She was bubbly and could keep up a conversation—though only about pop singers, like Pugacheva and Kirkorov—but she seemed nice enough. I couldn't make it to their wedding—I was spending all my time in the hospital with my mom. Zhenya went to Sergiyev Posad, the bride's hometown, hoping to put together a piece about the happy ending of a former prisoner of war. He came back emptyhanded, hungover, and in a foul mood: "There was nothing to shoot, only hopeless lowlifes. Everyone got drunk before the ceremony; they were too drunk even for a fight. The new family is planning to live in her grandmother's room in a communal apartment—once the grandmother dies. Everyone's looking forward to that happy occasion—when they would see off the young couple and live it up at the post-funeral gathering. Her parents? You should've seen them—typical provincial rubes. Only Kostya, the cameraman, and I were from the groom's side. But Kostya got drunk first, so you could say that I was the only one representing the groom on their special day." Something at the wedding had really rubbed Zhenya the wrong way, but I didn't ask any questions; there was too much going on.

After the wedding, Vadik would show up at the newspaper from time to time, traveling from Sergiyev Posad on two buses, a local train, and the metro. Then his visits became less frequent; he would show up only to borrow some money. But we hadn't been paid for three months, and Vadik gradually disappeared. A couple of times I tried to call the six-digit regional number he left, but no one answered.

No, he wasn't dead. There he was—Vadik.

"Stop shaking, Tanya! Let's figure out what's going on. We'll figure it out, then we'll start panicking. I'll check who called, and maybe you can find the video on the Internet, the one with Vadik. I want to see the entire thing. Okay, go already!"

There were nineteen unanswered calls from the previous three minutes. Okay, I know who this one is . . . and that one. An unknown number with a strange area code. Okay, we'll start with the important ones, then we'll move on.

"No, Mom, I don't understand what's going on yet. Yes, it's Vadik. I won't take any risks, don't worry. No, I can't talk to dad right now. I'll call you later, as soon as I learn anything new. Love you."

"Hi Misha. Why are you stressing out about all this? It's not worth it, it's all nonsense. You have a game tomorrow, and that's what you should be worrying about—not about me. Okay, I'll let you go, love you. And remember, you're the best Misha in the entire world. Of course, I'll call you before you go to sleep."

That's it, the home front was covered.

"I found the video," Tanya yelled from the other room. "Should I play it?"

The phone rang again—again the same unknown number with a strange area code.

"Wait, I'll just take this call and then we'll watch it."

"Pavel Vladimirovich?"

"Yes."

"This is Colonel Semyonov from the Federal Security Bureau. Have you heard the news?"

"I saw it on *Vesti* and I'm trying to make sense of it."

"Can we talk? I'm downstairs."

"I'll come down in fifteen minutes."

"Absolutely not! Call this number when you're ready, and I'll meet you outside your apartment."

Hostages, negotiators, a colonel from the FSB waiting for me at the door . . . Is this a soap opera? Or an insane asylum? Vadik, you bastard, what the fuck have you done? What did you get me into?

"Okay, let's watch the video."

Yes, it was definitely Vadik, there was no doubt about it. And he hadn't changed much. He used to be a little chubby, but now he was wiry. Another thing—Vadik didn't slouch anymore.

Sitting up straight and looking directly into the camera, Vadik announced to the whole world that he and his comrades had seized the church in the village of Nikolskoye. They had hostages—approximately a hundred people. For every movement in the vicinity of the church that seemed suspicious, they'd kill three people. Any attempt to storm the church— and they'd blow everybody up. They'd announce their demands to the negotiators they'd selected, the journalists Evgeny Styopin and Pavel Volodin, as soon as they arrive at the site. That was it for now. More to come.

He didn't say: We'll *execute* the hostages, just "kill"—and in the matter of fact, business-like tone of someone who's in a hurry and afraid to leave out something important and so is very focused.

Everything was clear. Actually, nothing was clear. Either Vadik had lost his mind or . . . The only thing that was clear was that it was time for me to call Colonel Semyonov and leave.

"I'll figure everything out there. Should I call Zhenya? No, I won't, we'll talk when I see him. I'm ready, Colonel."

"Wait!" Tanya shouts. "Never mind, I'm fine. Everything's gonna be okay. I just got dizzy for a second. Listen . . . Be careful over there, okay? If something happens to you, you know I won't survive."

We drove down some side streets, through some industrial parks in Bibirevo—I'd been living in that neighborhood for twenty years and had no idea you could go this way. We got onto the Moscow Ring Road in less than seven minutes.

"By the way, what does all this have to do with the FSB? And can you tell me what's happening in Nikolskoye?"

"I have my orders: to deliver you—you're now under our protection, the rest is above my pay grade. I can turn on the radio, if you want."

"That'd be great. Can you find the station Golos?"

There were three people on the air—two journalists and the editor-in-chief. Good for him, a real professional; he'd left his evening whiskey, run to the studio, and gotten on the microphone. When things get that bad, of course the editor-in-chief needs to be on the air. His voice was trembling with excitement. Yes, we journalists experience a certain bloodlust every time something out of the ordinary happens. On the one hand, it's misery and horror. On the other—it's the essence of our work, when everyone's running around like crazy, everything's spinning and rotating, you're pulled in all directions, and it makes you happy—it's nothing like the moldy news we chew on day after day. Okay, let's hear it: What had they dug up?

By that time, they hadn't dug up very much, nothing more than *Vesti*, only without any pictures. Due to the late hour, they were able to find only one commentator—Belkovsky, the station errand boy—who offered fresh thoughts on the inability of the government to confront modern challenges, in particular, terrorist threats.

"As for the people the hostage takers want as their negotiators . . ." I got ready to listen to my own biography.

There was little doubt how Lyosha would begin, and he didn't disappoint: "Well, the negotiations will be handled by our colleagues, one of whom is a friend of our program, having been on Golos numerous times. We've worked together for years. He was the host of a program on our radio station." If Lyosha hadn't taken advantage of the situation to advertise his show, I would have thought he was seriously ill. "Why these negotiators were chosen, we don't know yet, but we will definitely contact Styopin and Volodin and bring them on the air so our listeners, as always, will be the first to know." I imagined him stepping out of the studio for a second to scream at his assistants: "I gave you their numbers, you idiots! If he doesn't answer, call Vasina—he must be in contact with her, for sure. Get a hold of him—I need him on the air!" No, not right now, Lyosha. I wish someone would explain to me what was going on.

At the exit to Vidnoye from the Kashirskoye highway, you could see the first signs that something was going on in the area. Police cars with flashing lights were posted every five hundred meters. Next to them, there were units of riot police and SWAT teams, and the road to Nikolskoye was blocked by two police trucks parked parallel to each other. No one had asked for our papers before that—it seems our plates were enough, but here, our driver was stopped for the first time; he rolled down his window and showed his ID to the officer in charge. We repeated the same ritual when entering Nikolskoye, but now our driver's ID wasn't enough, and everybody had to show their papers, including Colonel Semyonov. It wasn't the police who were manning this checkpoint. It was the people in civilian clothes that spent the most time studying my passport.

They set up headquarters in the only local store. Between shelves filled with canned goods, beer, and chips, they'd placed two plastic tables and a few plastic chairs. At the table sat six men—all of them brutish and well-fed. No one was wearing a uniform, but it was clear they were high ranking. Only one man was a civilian—from the ministry of health, as we learned later, the rest were representatives of the various security forces—the MVD, FSB, and MChS—the national guard, and one from the local police. We could have held a parade. Everyone wore the same facial expression, a mixture of annoyance, anger, and fear. Of course, they'd all been summoned from their holiday celebrations, and at the most inopportune moment, after they'd filled their first shot glass, even their second, and were beginning to feel relaxed and even happy. They'd sat down to eat and were getting ready for that coveted third shot, in honor of the fallen, when the phone rang.

And suddenly they had to drop everything and rush off in the middle of the night to God knows where. Well, they knew where they were going, but no one understood what the hell had happened. "Some idiots!" "A hundred plus hostages inside a church." "They're not saying what they want." "Are they Chechens?" "The guy in the Internet video looked like a Slav." In short, the evening was completely ruined, but that was just half their problem. They'd have to deal with all the mess, and if something went wrong, they'd be held responsible. "And here's this negotiator—who knows who the hell he is." All this was written on their faces clear as day. Although you probably wouldn't say that I looked happy to see them either.

"This is Volodin," Colonel Semyonov explained. "Come in, have a seat. Where's the other one?" asked a man in a suit and tie. They must have brought him straight from work—his morning shirt wasn't looking too fresh. The rest of them were dressed in whatever, but definitely their civilian clothes; only one guy from MChS was wearing camouflage. "We're still looking for him," Semyonov replied. "No luck so far. They said he went out partying." It will take you all night to find him, I thought. If Zhenya has really decided to go partying, he won't be easy to find. Before, considering the circumstances, I would've probably helped you out and given you his address, now I don't have a clue—I haven't heard from him in five years, and I couldn't even guess where he hangs out now.

"Okay, let's not waste any time. It all started four hours ago."

At 7 P.M., two men approached three police officers who'd arrived in their jeep to patrol the church premises over the holiday. One of the men reached into his pocket and pulled out a hand grenade with the pin already removed and shouted: "On the ground, face down, arms in front of you, or I'll blow everybody up." They took the policemen's weapons and their police radio, put them in their own handcuffs and led two of the policemen toward the church, where you could hear screaming. They said to the third one: "Run and tell your bosses that we'll soon have more than a hundred hostages. If you try to shoot in our direction, we'll kill three people for every shot. And if you try to storm the church, we have enough explosives to blow up everyone. All the details are on YouTube. And now, clear out." The grenade, which happened to be fake, was thrown into a ditch.

That lucky policeman ran to the nearest house and

informed the authorities. An hour later there were national guard troops surrounding the village, and the police had closed the road, special forces had encircled the church, and the nearby houses had been evacuated. The remaining villagers were warned not to step foot outside their homes, but the relatives of the hostages gathered around the administration building and refused to leave. There were about thirty local people in the church, the rest were from nearby villages and housing developments. No one knew the exact number of hostages, but it seemed like it was more than a hundred. No one knew what was happening inside. It was quiet over there. No one left the church. The surrounding premises were illuminated by floodlights installed on the roof by the attackers. How many of them were there? No one knew that either. They were trying to establish the identity of the man from the YouTube video.

They hadn't done anything else yet; they were waiting for Zhenya and me to be brought in. By that time, they knew two things about me: my place of work and my address. "Do you have any idea who the attackers are? What do they want? And why did they choose you two in particular?"

"I don't know who they are, but I sure know who this man is—no need for you to worry about his identity. He's Vadim Petrovich Seryogin. He goes by Vadik. Here's what I know about him, at least about his first nineteen years: He was born in Novomoskovsk, where he was recruited into the army. He fought in Chechnya, was captured, and spent half a year as a prisoner of war. Zhenya and I rescued him. He lived in Moscow after that. The last I knew of him he was living in Sergiev Posad with his wife. When did I see him last? About sixteen years ago, I don't remember exactly. He chose Styopin and me simply because he doesn't know anyone else—I don't have any other explanation. Well, he probably trusts us too."

"Extremism, terrorism, any criminal activity?"

"Who, Vadik? Not in a million years—he's always been quiet as a mouse."

When the questioning was over, I started to feel depressed. Before, with all the commotion, I'd managed somehow. But now, when it was clear that this was it, there was no escape—I would have to go to that church to see Vadik and his mysterious comrades, and most likely, I'd have to go alone because the FSB appeared incapable of finding out where Zhenya was—I got so scared that I wanted to ask for something to calm my nerves and then, under the pretext of feeling sick, I spent an additional fifteen minutes in the store. On the other hand, I thought, Anna Politkovskaya was a negotiator in Dubrovka, and in Budyonovsk journalists sat in the same bus with Basayev, and Ruslan Aushev was there, in the Beslan school, and even rescued some children. When it comes down to it, they already have enough hostages and now they need negotiators. And why would Vadik kill me? He's never seen anything but kindness from me. Whatever you say, damn, it's a real shock . . . Vadik.

Oh, well, there was no getting out of it. I'd have to go.

"Semyonov will take you there," said the man in the rumpled shirt. Yes, of course, let Semyonov take me there. I'll even show him the way.

A long time ago, Valera Silantiev, who grew up in Lytkarino, showed me the church in Nikolskoye. Back in his childhood, he and some other guys from the opposite bank of the Moscow River would swim over to the church, although back then it wasn't much, just a dilapidated skeleton. But even so, the ruins made an impression. Of course, I'm not an expert on old Russian architecture, but it was really beautiful.

Before all the dams and reservoirs, when the Moscow River would flood in the spring, water would cut off Nikolskoye from the rest of the world. The church was built on the highest point, right above the beginning of the flood plain. And the view from the bell tower extended at least ten kilometers. If you ignored the cooling towers of the power plant in Dzerzhinsky, the view was spectacular. You could see the fields and the hills between Lytkarino and Vidnoye and other churches on the opposite bank of the Moscow River. And the church itself was very attractive. I've never seen architecture like that anywhere else—sharp lines, hard corners, nothing was smooth, but the impression it created was one of lightness, airiness, dapper elegance. It looked more like a mosque than an Orthodox church.

I used to go to Nikolskoye often—on spring vacation, or in early September when it was still hot, or just for weekends. It was so close, only thirty minutes by the Ring Road, but the place was exceptional. There were views, and the church, and you could get to the river through the meadow. The dogs were happy, and, as a rule, the girls liked it too. Places like this are meant to be shared, and I used to drag everyone I liked there.

When *Moskovsky Kuryer* became a joint-stock company and we had to decide how to celebrate this historic event, I suggested that we not waste money on pretentious restaurants, but instead, buy something to drink, marinate some meat for a barbeque and organize a picnic. It was May and the weather was gorgeous. That must have been the first time Vadik saw Nikolskoye and the church. Naturally, we took Vadik with us—wasn't he part of the gang?

That picnic turned out great, even though going public didn't help us much—the newspaper folded six years later.

We rented two buses and reached Nikolskoye around noon. The weather was warm, almost hot. We set up our grills, had something to eat and drink, and then I took everyone who was interested on a tour of the church, retelling Valera's stories about the underground path that was supposedly three kilometers long and ended at the river. Vadik went with us.

At that time of year, darkness comes so late it feels like there won't be any night at all.

Tanya travelled to the picnic on the bus with the others. I took my car, and so I didn't drink. It was everything a celebration should be. Toasts were made to the success of *Moskovsky Kuryer*, in particular, and to freedom of speech, in general. I played soccer with the guys. Tanya hung out with the women. Then she asked: "Do you have that key with you?" My heart skipped a beat.

Three days before the picnic, I got the key to a studio apartment in Marino from my buddy Palych and told Tanya about it: "Here it is . . . Well, if you . . . then I . . . basically, I love you, and none of that's important, of course . . . but . . . yes, I love you."

We didn't tell anyone anything, we didn't even say goodbye,

so later they launched an all-out search for us. But we didn't learn about that until the next day. We didn't just drive to Marino, we flew there—and then froze in the hallway of the dusty unoccupied apartment. We stood for a long time, hugging.

"We're not in a hurry, right?" "Right, we're already here." "You . . . you . . . you . . ." "And you . . ." "Wait, I need to take a shower . . . and you too, the soccer champion. I watched you playing, and you know what I thought?" "Yes, that's right, and you too? Just wait." "Five minutes." "Please!" "No, that's not how you unbutton it. Let me do it." "Oh, God!"

O h, God, the things that come into my head! "Let's go, Colonel. Let's go."

Only when we were outside did I realize that I'd never been in Nikolskoye at night. Usually, we'd come in the morning or early afternoon and then leave before dark. But now it was total darkness—the streetlights were off, only the windows glimmered behind tightly closed curtains, and you could see the dimmed parking lights of the police cars and military vehicles. We were walking down those familiar streets, trying to avoid puddles, while two troopers in black camouflage with machine guns across their chests walked in front of us. We reached the church cemetery where they had set up the last checkpoint, and four troopers in the same black uniforms moved away from the fence and approached us:

"What's going on?" asked one of the troopers who was accompanying us.

"Everything's quiet, Comrade Major. No one has come out, there hasn't been any noise—we've been listening."

"And the windows?"

"It's a church—the openings are narrow and deep, and the spotlights are blinding us, so we can't see anything. But they're watching us."

"Of course. Do you think they put out any tripwires?"

"We don't know. Well, we'll know more when the negotiators arrive."

"Quiet. This is one of the negotiators."

"Oops! Sorry, I thought he was someone from headquarters."

"Think less. Dismissed."

That trooper was sincerely sorry and was truly embarrassed, and somehow his embarrassment suddenly calmed me down, even my trembling stopped—I'd been seized by a violent shaking during our walk from the store to the church.

"Good luck to you," the major said.

"If something . . ." Semyonov began to say.

"If something what?"

"I don't know," he answered abruptly.

It was time to go. If I kept standing there, the guys would realize how scared I was. Although, they probably had some idea already. The hell with them! It's not like they were willing to switch places with me. So, here I go.

One night a taxi driver told me a story. In his youth, he'd worked in construction as a high rigger. One day, the scaffold collapsed, and he went flying from three stories up, trying to grab hold of anything within reach to stop the fall. "You know, they say that in situations like this your entire life flashes before your eyes. That's bull," the taxi driver assured me. "Not a single scene. It's all a bunch of lies, or else there was nothing in my life worth remembering."

That's right. I didn't see a single scene either.

I walked along the cemetery fence until I reached the gate to the church. I pushed it open and stopped at the border between light and darkness, where the light from the projectors installed on the roof ended. I was standing there thinking: "Those bastards, it's not enough that you took people as hostages, you didn't even bother to tell us where to go. Though, precise instructions aren't strictly necessary—there aren't too many options here."

I walked twenty more steps and stopped in front of a heavy ironclad door. There were people inside. A lot of people. They were quiet, but it's impossible for more than a hundred people not to make a sound, especially if there are children. They weren't even crying, just whining like puppies that want to go outside; the women tried quietly to hush them. I pulled the iron ring and opened the door:

"Hello, Vadik."

He was standing in the aisle and smiling. In the same way he was smiling eighteen years ago when we returned to Makhkety to get him. Zhenya and I were walking down the street toward Lechi's house, and Vadik stood near the gate and watched us approach. When we arrived . . . perhaps, children in an orphanage smile in the same way when they're told they're about to leave to live with a family—they smile happily but with some mistrust. Anyway, what do I know, having never adopted anyone from an orphanage. I'd never even visited one. I couldn't bring myself to go.

"Hello, Uncle Pasha."

How many times had we tried to get him to stop calling us Uncle Pasha and Uncle Zhenya, but to no avail? He would get confused for a second and then just skip our names all together, referring to us impersonally or with a prolonged "E-e-eh," just like Evgeny Alexeyevich Kiselyev when he loses his train of thought. Well, you can take the boy out of Novomoskovsk . . .

There was a strong smell of sweat in the church. Not the sweat of a locker room after a game, when two dozen men happily strip off their jerseys. This was the smell of fear-induced sweat, the smell of horror.

"Where's Uncle Zhenya?"

Who the hell knows where your Uncle Zhenya is? I hope the special services have finally gotten a hold of him and are bringing him here, so I'm not the only one facing death.

"He'll be here soon. They're looking for him."

"Partying on the holidays, huh?"

"Something like that. You know Zhenya."

"So, he's still the same?"

Vadik and I were having such a friendly conversation, like between relatives. As if, let's say, a nephew who'd moved away many years ago looking for work, returned home and asked his elderly uncle about the family. But what was I supposed to do? Give him a lecture? Do you realize, Mr. Seryogin, the possible implications of your unlawful actions?

"Yeah, he's still the same. Probably. I haven't seen him in a long time."

"Did you have a fight?"

No, we didn't have a fight, we just went our separate ways. After we brought Vadik to Moscow, Zhenya and I became best friends—"drunk" as thieves, as Zhenya used to say. Together we went on two more out-of-town assignments, to South Ossetia and Karabakh, and made documentaries about life in these unrecognized republics following the victory of their national liberation movements. We were planning to go to Abkhazia too but never made it there; we got bored seeing the same thing everywhere—yesterday's heroes were lying in the cemetery or had turned into real gangsters; the population was miserable and living in fear; there was poverty and devastation everywhere, but at least all the signs were now written in the national language. We went to independent Chechnya too and saw our interlocuter Basayev in charge of the local customs office. I've never seen anything funnier in my life. But in truth, there were few spectacles more terrifying.

And then another life began. The Second Chechen War, building explosions, then Yeltsin left and Putin came, launching his "Save Russia" campaign.

I called him once: "Zhenya, let's go on a tour of all the old, familiar places." I could tell he wasn't too eager. Back then I didn't pay much attention—there could be all kinds of things going on in his life. Then Zhenya left Vidy Sovremennosti and stopped coming to the building on Petrovka Street. Well, I had enough problems of my own. The next thing I hear is that he went to work for Channel One. I hadn't seen his pieces, but the guys told me: "Zhenya's filming only priests and generals now, that whole Russia getting up from its knees and, blessed with the cross, sending its armies to fight the sacred fight." "Who, Zhenya?! Come on!" "Watch for yourself!"

The last time we saw each other was seven years ago, when Zhenya invited us to his house-warming party. The apartment was awesome—huge, in an old Stalin-era building near Ostankino, with euro-remodeling, and recessed ceilings. "Very cool," I said. "You've got a great set-up, and you can walk to work now."

"But wait," Zhenya responded. "Let's go outside. You've got to see what I'm driving now." There was a new Saab in the courtyard: a two-and-a-half-liter engine, leather seats, the works—every man's dream.

"You're really coming up in the world."

"I was doing a piece in Yekaterinburg," Zhenya told me. "The local guys gave up on the police and took the fight against drugs into their own hands. They'd gather together, take bats, metal rods, what have you, and go to the homes of the gypsies where they sell the drugs: 'You leave our city, or we'll burn down your houses.' It was a great piece, pure adrenaline. The guys loved the piece so much, they gave me this Saab as a thank you."

Yes, I heard about those guys in Yekaterinburg. They were from the Uralmash gang and among the first to realize that times had changed. No more small actions; it was time to go legit and start building up political capital. Someone was later found dead in a prison, while someone else survived—and thrived.

"And you accepted it?"

"Why wouldn't I? It's a noble cause—fighting narcotraffickers."

We haven't seen each other since then, just an occasional phone call.

"No, we didn't really have a fight. Well, when they find Zhenya, you can ask him yourself. So, start talking already."

"Okay, so we're holding one hundred and twelve people—twelve children and exactly one hundred adults, if you count cops as people."

"And what do you want?"

"I'll explain later, when Uncle Zhenya shows up. So, I don't have to get up twice, as you put it."

He's got a good memory, who would've thought. I really do like that expression and even remember where I got it from—I read it in something by Viktor Semenovich.

"So what? When he shows up, you'll repeat it."

"No, let's wait for Uncle Zhenya."

"Fine. Any injured?"

"No, everyone's fine."

"Let's ask if anyone needs medication. There must be people with heart problems or diabetes."

"We've already asked. They don't need anything. We have valocordin and insulin."

Well, I'll be darned. Vadik correctly pronounced *valocordin* and *insulin*, and what's more, he knew what they're used for—this was truly impressive, like seeing a talking dog.

"Do you have any water?"

"We have everything—food and water."

"What about bathrooms?"

"We found a bucket and take them out one at a time."

They corralled everyone who'd come that evening for services into the middle of the church, ordering them to sit on the floor and look down. They must have been very convincing—

not a single person looked up when we came in, not even any of the children. The attackers were stationed one in each corner—near the entrance and in front of the altar—to watch the hostages, and there were two near the windows, to watch outside. It's possible there were more, but I saw only those six. Plus Vadik. All of them were armed with short Kalashnikovs. They didn't hide their faces. There was water inside, they hadn't lied about that: several five-liter containers near the wall. "What food do you have?" "There's bread, two boxes." Right! And you've already provided the circuses.

"Okay, let's get out of here. Want some tea?"

At that moment, more than anything else in the world, I wanted some cognac, at least two hundred millimeters to start with. Or let them tell me that all this was just a nightmare, a delusion, a hallucination. If someone were to tell me that, I wouldn't touch a drop of alcohol ever again. I swear.

And amid the stench and the quiet sobbing, I definitely didn't want to drink his tea.

"Sure."

We went to a storage closet—a small, windowless room used to store mops, brooms, and buckets—flipped over two of the buckets, and sat down. Vadik got the tea and some sugar and turned on the electric teapot. He was totally calm and unhurried. You'd think taking hostages was an everyday job for him. It suddenly occurred to me: Who the hell knows what's in his heart. What had he been doing all the time I didn't hear from him? Even before he disappeared, I didn't know much about him—Vadik was just . . . well, Vadik, like a stray dog you take in from the street.

"How've you been doing, Uncle Pasha?"

That is a very good question, Vadik. Thank you so much for asking. I used to think my life was so-so, but now, with your help, I realize that everything before tonight was so wonderful, it would be a sin to complain.

"Not bad, I guess."

"How are you parents? Still alive?"

"Yeah, they're alive, but their health isn't great."

"Did you marry Tatyana?"

Our affair wasn't a secret to anyone at the newspaper and, naturally, Vadik had heard all the gossip from the secretaries and in the accounting and proofing departments. We kept getting together, breaking up, quarreling again, then making up again . . . It went on like that for five years—she just couldn't bring herself to tell her kid about me. How idiotic! Or was I the idiot for not insisting on it?

"Yes, I got married. The first time, to someone else. Then I married Tatyana."

"Any children?"

"A son. He's fourteen. He lives with his mother half the time, the other half, with us.

"Is he a good kid?"

"Well, I like him."

"How are things at work?"

What can I tell you? I probably shouldn't go into detail about how we were let go from *Moskovsky Kuryer* and how those people you used to know reacted to that . . . How we've been hustling since then . . . and what a dirty business journalism has become . . . What do you need to know all that for? Would it even mean anything to you?

"Everything's okay. It's a long story. But what about you?"

Everything was going okay for Vadik, too. That's what he said.

While waiting for the grandma to die and free up her room in the communal apartment, Vadik and Nina lived with her parents. (Right, her name was Nina, I couldn't remember.) It was a normal life. At night Vadik would have a drink or two with his father-in-law and listen to his army stories while his mother-in-law and Nina would watch TV. On weekends they'd go to the Ikea that had recently opened in Khimki. They didn't have money to buy anything, but it was nice to look around.

It wasn't easy to find a job in the town of Sergiev Posad, and the only position he could get was as a garbage truck assistant. The driver opens the back flap, and the assistant rolls up the garbage container and secures it so it can be emptied into the truck. Then he rolls the container back to its place and cleans up any leftover garbage with a shovel. The pay wasn't bad, and it was always on time. The only negative thing was that you stank after a shift. So, Nina's mother insisted that, before entering the apartment, Vadik change in the hallway, put his work clothes in a plastic bag, and take the bag out onto the balcony.

Nina was selling vegetables at a small store. She turned out to be not as flaky as she seemed. She found some free accounting courses and signed up; the classes were twice a week. And she ordered Vadik: "Don't drink, please, or our kid will be born with defects." "What kid? Don't you have to get pregnant first?" But such counterarguments didn't work with her: "Don't drink, end of discussion."

The accounting courses were not in Sergiev Posad but in the neighboring town of Alexandrovo. Nina would return home on the last train, and Vadik would meet her at the station.

Everything happened because of that.

Once in November, Vadik was stopped by a police patrol— a sergeant and two soldiers.

"Your ID, please."

"Oh, crap, I left it at home."

"Pay five hundred rubles, and you're free."

"Guys, I don't even have a twenty. I left in a hurry to meet my wife."

"Then you'll have to come with us, and we'll find out who you are."

"Come on, guys, it's not cool . . ."

"And you're drunk in public. That's it, we're taking you to the station to file a report."

"Can I at least wait for my wife? She'll worry if I'm not here."

At that moment, Nina appeared. Vadik explained the situation, and she proposed to the policemen: "I can go get his ID." They stepped to the side to discuss her proposition. "Okay, go," they said. "But our shift is over, and we can't just let him go, so you'll have to bring his ID to the station."

On the way to the station, they shared a bottle of vodka in the car, neighing like horses the whole time.

"Okay, listen up," the sergeant said. "She's brought your ID, but it turns out, you're not registered in this city." Vadik tried to explain that it was all his mother-in-law's fault: "She didn't want me to have any right to their apartment, and so she would tell Nina: 'Who knows if things will work out between you two, but when the room is free, you can register him then.'"

"This is a violation of regulations," the sergeant informed him. "The penalty is seven hundred rubles. But that's not your biggest problem. You were drunk in a public place—but that's still not the worst thing. You resisted arrest—that's serious."

"How did I resist arrest?!"

"Whatever we say, goes. Who do you think the judge will believe tomorrow, the police or a homeless person? In short, you could easily get two years. But we can end this to our mutual satisfaction . . ."

They then proposed the following to Vadik: "Convince your woman to go to the back room and entertain us, sexually, it can be just a blowjob, and there won't be any report. You'll walk out of here a free man."

Vadik attacked, but there were three of them . . . When he came to, he was in a cell. In the morning new officers arrived. "Why are you lying around here?" they asked. He tried to explain to them what had happened, but no one listened. "Get out of here. Go!" He barely made it home. And for the next three days, he had blood in his urine because they had damaged his kidneys.

Two months later, Nina hanged herself. Her father had a garage even though he didn't have a car. They used the garage for storage, to keep potatoes, and that's where she did it.

After beating up Vadik and throwing him in a cell, the cops told her: "Here's the deal. Your guy attacked us for no reason, almost killed us, he was probably drunk, or high. He's looking now at five years, minimum. But we're not bad people, we understand. So, you lift up your skirt, and you can pick him up in the morning. It'll be over in half an hour." She started crying and then agreed. They filmed it all and showed it to anyone who wanted to see. In a week's time, all of Sergiev Posad knew. It's a small town—so when you walk down the street, the old women whisper, the boys giggle. Well, she couldn't take it. After her death, Vadik told everything to an investigator, they even opened a case, but no arrests followed. In the video, only she was recognizable, no other faces were in the frame.

Then Vadik took a metal rod, sharpened it on one end, and wrapped the other with duct tape. He had already found out where the sergeant from that patrol lived. After all, Sergiev Pasad is not a big city, everybody knows everything about everybody—the good things and the bad. It was clear that he wouldn't be able to get all three of them, so he had to choose.

Vadik followed the sergeant on his way home from work through a vacant lot and hit him on the back of the head with a brick. The policeman dropped to the ground. Vadik had imagined it many times: how he would kill him—slowly, very slowly . . . But when Vadik saw his eyes—the sergeant came to and recognized him—he felt only disgust and sadness. Vadik hit him several times in the face with the metal rod, then in the neck—he squealed like a pig at first, then fell silent. Vadik went straight to the bus station and left the city. He reached his destination in a week. What was his destination? Chechnya, of course.

He escaped to Makhkety, traveling with truck drivers and on minibuses, sometimes he walked, but always avoided those places where he might run into cops. He had had enough of those interactions. He reached Chechnya at just the right time.

# THE SUMMER OF 1999

I t happened in the summer of 1999.
In Chechnya that summer everyone was discussing the news that Shamil Basayev was preparing for a military campaign in Dagestan and that there would be a new war. In Grozny, the farmer's market, the most reliable source of information, confirmed the news: there was a sudden jump in the price of guns and ammunition.

Everything happened exactly as people were saying. In August, Basayev organized a regiment and headed through the mountains to the Daghestani villages of Karamakhi and Chabanmakhi. To protect his brothers in faith, as he announced.

In these villages, back in the Soviet days, people lived pretty well. The soil was fertile, and there was plenty of it. The locals grew vegetables and watermelons and took them to markets in Russia. In Soviet times, they paid protection money to the police, then some criminal gangs arrived from Makhachkala, which didn't mean the police left, only that everyone now wanted a cut. Meanwhile, vegetables from Turkey found their way into the Russian markets, with prices so cheap the local farmers couldn't compete. Business was over.

In addition, new people were moving to Karamakhi and Chabanmakhi, and these people would gather in the evening to study the Koran. They would say: Life must be lived justly, as Allah teaches, no drinking, no smoking, respect for elders, women must know their place, along with many other rules. And any authorities that get in the way are against God and should not be tolerated. The local people listened and obeyed. They kicked out the criminal gangs first, then the cops, and finally, the government bureaucrats and the judges. Life under Sharia law had begun. The nineties were reaching their peak, the whole country was turned upside down, and the situation in Dagestan was even worse, so no one had the time or the energy to deal with the godforsaken villages of Karamakhi and Chabanmakhi. They lived peacefully, didn't bother anyone, and that was good enough for the moment. Dealing with Chechnya was a much higher priority.

When the situation with Chechnya had stabilized some-what, the government remembered Karamakhi and Chabanmakhi. What's going on over there? Are these centers of religious fanatism? Are there Wahabis? Is it anarchy?

What happened next is a total mystery. Some said that after being pressured by the authorities, the people of Karamakhi and Chabanmakhi asked Basayev for help, and he didn't refuse, especially as one of his wives was from the area. Others were of the opinion that Shamil couldn't care less about all these brothers-in-faith, and that his major goal was to annoy Maskhadov and provoke the Russians into fighting. Then Basayev would replace Maskhadov as the people's hero. Still others whispered that Basayev began his campaign in the summer of 1999 not for free, but was paid by Berezovsky, who wanted another war so that Putin could claim victory and then be elected president.

No one could prove anything for sure, but one fact was certain—Vadik made it back just in time.

Vadik had hoped to work for Lechi Sultygov, but he'd been killed by then. Thanks to Zhenya, Lechi had become famous in Chechnya and quickly made a career for himself—after Maskhadov became president, he made Lechi head of security in the Shalinsky region. But other people had hoped to secure that position, and very soon Lechi, along with two of his bodyguards, was blown up in his car. After the war, show-downs among the Chechen clans began in earnest . . .

Lechi's younger brother Ruslan, who'd become head of the family, had nothing against Vadik and let him live with them. His only question was: "What did you do?" Vadik told the truth. Ruslan nodded with approval. They gave him a place in the same barn where he'd been held captive, but now he worked around the house with the others as an equal and ate at the family table. He didn't worry much about being on the most wanted list—the nearest cops, or any other Russian authorities for that matter, were in far-away Stavropol.

Everything went back to normal, but then, suddenly, there was another war.

A nd what happened next?"

"I think it's time for you to go."

"Yes, it's about time. What should I tell them at head-quarters?"

"Nothing's changed: Don't shoot. Don't attack. Wait for our demands. We'll let you know as soon as they bring Uncle Zhenya. I didn't show you how we organized it all here, but tell them, if they decide to attack, it wouldn't be like in Dubrovka. It'll be more like Beslan, but worse."

"I'll tell them. Will you release the children?"

"No," Vadik answered in a matter-of-fact tone.

Outside, I stopped and lit a cigarette—it hadn't felt right to smoke in the church.

Being in a hurry, I'd forgotten to ask my men in black about the protocol for exiting. Not in the sense of where to go, but how to avoid being mistaken for someone else and shot. Those professionals, of course, didn't tell me anything. Oh, well, let's hope they have night vision devices and are able to tell the difference between me and a terrorist. After all, aren't they special forces?"

They were waiting for me at the same spot, and Semyonov was with them—naturally, as I was now under their protection.

While I was away, the headquarters had been moved from the store to the village administrative offices. All roads leading to that building were clogged with cars—with and without flashing lights, and with license plates of the most privileged kind, from the government and special forces. It was a total circus. Inside, the same people were waiting for me, except for one new man—in an expensive suit, with angry eyes. He'd been sent from the president's office. Of course, that's what we'd been missing all this time! But there was some good news too: They'd found Zhenya, and he'd be here in twenty minutes. I wondered if Zhenya would be pleased.

"So, how did it go?"

I told them about what I'd seen: the hostages, the terrorists, the weapons, and the food. I decided to keep what Vadik had told me to myself for now, as it wasn't their business, at least, not yet. I needed to reflect on it a little longer myself. They knew Vadik's last name, I'd told them that, so they must have already looked him up in their databases and knew that he was on the most-wanted list, and for what. They would learn the rest later . . .

"Who are they?"

"The ones I saw weren't Chechens, and I think they're not even from the Caucasus region."

"Are they Russians?"

"Their faces are Slavic."

"How old?"

"They're young."

"What did you agree to—what's happening next?"

"After Zhenya arrives, Seryogin will tell us what they want. For some reason it's important to him that we're together. I don't understand why."

And there he was, our long-awaited friend. I'd seen him looking better, that's for sure. He hadn't shaved for probably three days, his hair was all messed up, his hands were shaking, and his eyes were cloudy and unfocused; they reminded me of my dog's eyes when he doesn't want to go back home after a walk. Someone should probably give him a drink, for starters.

"It's amazing they were able to find you, Zhenya. I thought it would be an impossible task."

"Yeah, right. It would have been better if they hadn't. Have you seen Vadik? What, has he lost his mind?"

"It doesn't seem so. You can see for yourself soon."

"I'm not going anywhere, I already told them! I won't talk to that asshole!"

"He doesn't want to give us their demands without you there."

"He can go to hell with his demands! Why should I do this? By the way, I have two children, actually, three."

"Why did you come here then?"

"They said I had to."

This was strange. Zhenya may be a lot of things, but he's never been a coward. To be more precise, he was a gambler, and his risk-taking didn't allow him to be frightened, even in the most unpleasant situations—I'd witnessed it myself. But then again, people change.

"I'm sorry, we need to talk. Zhenya, let's go for a smoke." We walked out into the hallway and stood near the window.

"Don't you understand? There are more than a hundred people sitting and staring at the floor, taking turns pissing in a bucket, there are children . . ."

"And how can we help them? By listening to his idiotic demands?"

"Well, yes . . ."

"As if I don't know what bullshit he's going to say: Freedom to Chechnya, withdraw the troops, all that nonsense."

"Why do you think so?"

"Why? Why? Because! I didn't tell you back then. When I went to his wedding in . . . what's the town?"

"Sergiev Posad."

"Right. He got really drunk and told me a lot of stuff. In Chechnya, he wasn't a prisoner of war, he went there of his own free will, with a weapon."

"Why?"

"He said he was often bullied in his army unit. But I think he's just a son of a bitch. Because the Chechens made one demand: prove you're not a spy by converting to Islam. And he agreed. After his dick healed, they told him: 'Since you're one of us now, let's attack the Russian convoy. And so, he went. He told me he didn't shoot, that they didn't give him a weapon, that he was only reloading machine guns. But I don't believe him."

So that's how it was. I wondered who was lying. Vadik? Or Zhenya, to work himself up? I wouldn't put it past Zhenya; he had a formidable imagination. But maybe no one was lying and all of this was true. But really, what difference did it make?

"Okay, let's assume that's all true. What do you suggest? That we don't go, that we don't listen to them? That we wait until we have another Beslan? Don't you know who you're dealing with? They'll kill everyone, even the children, just to show off how cool they are."

"This is a war, Pasha! A war! People die during wars, unfortunately."

"And who's fighting who, I wonder? But if you don't want to go, then don't. I'll go alone."

"What are you, an idiot?! They're not going to release any of them. Chernomyrdin's not the prime minister anymore, so we can't just ask Shamil Basayev to speak up, please. In any scenario, they're doomed."

"And the hostages?"

"What about the hostages? They'll save as many of them as they can."

Well, I thought to myself, who's the real son of a bitch here?

"Okay, we're through. I'm going."

Up to the last possible moment, I waited for him to change his mind. I hadn't waited like that for anything in a very long time. Maybe never. That's how much I didn't want to go back into that church, but even more, I didn't want to make any decisions alone. No luck, Zhenya had made up his mind. He remained standing in the same spot, looking through the window into the darkness. He didn't even turn his head. What an asshole, to abandon a friend! Or was I the asshole for having friends like him?

Before I left, the man from the president's office tried to lecture me: "Don't be too soft with them. Don't let them feel that they can get away with this. Act from a position of power." Fucking politician. "Would you like to come with me?" I asked. "I'm a little absent-minded and may forget some of your valuable instructions."

By the time I arrived back at the church, the stench had gotten worse, and the mournful sobbing had grown quieter. Some of them had probably fallen asleep from exhaustion.

No, Vadik, Uncle Zhenya's not coming. Your touching reunion has been postponed until better times. He didn't want to give you a hug.

"He probably told you?"

"What exactly?"

"Well, about me . . ."

"Yes, he told me. Is it true?"

"Yes. I wanted to explain it to him back then but couldn't. I was too drunk. And so was he."

"Why didn't you tell *me* back then?"

"I thought Uncle Zhenya would tell you."

"Okay, but what difference does it make now? Now we need to . . ."

I honestly had no idea what we needed to do now. But realistically, what could possibly be done? So, Vadik, now that everyone else is out of the picture, tell me all your crazy ideas. Go ahead, don't be shy, it seems like there's no other audience left. Perhaps, an investigator will be interested, but that's if you're really lucky . . . and not just you.

"It's too bad, Uncle Zhenya didn't come. But I won't be talking. Here, read this."

He took a piece of paper folded in four from the front

pocket of his shirt. It was written by hand, it seemed, a long time ago and had been reread many times since—the edges were tattered. Okay, give me your manuscript, genius.

"We demand," that's how the declaration began.

"You're not thinking straight, Vadik," I said after I finished reading. "Do you seriously believe *he* would go for this?"

"I don't know. What do you think?"

"I think there's not a chance. None whatsoever."

"Well, no means no."

"What next?"

"Next? There won't be anything next. They'll try to break in. We'll blow up the place. And that'll be the end."

"You're not afraid to die?"

"I am afraid. But I can't go on. I don't want to go on."

"Can you explain why you needed to do all this?"

"I can."

It was all very simple. And absolutely hopeless.

"Just don't try to talk me out of it, Uncle Pasha. And don't ask me if I feel sorry about the hostages. Don't waste your time," Vadik said before I even started talking. He said it in such a way that my words stuck in my throat. As if he'd cocked his gun.

"Listen carefully, Vadik. The situation is bad. For everyone. For you, for me, for the people you've taken hostage. But I think there's a chance. A small one, but still a chance. To take advantage of it, I'll need to go to Moscow to prepare everything, and then I'll come back in the morning. I'll tell the guys at headquarters that you need time to think. Let's say, until 10 A.M. Is that okay?"

"To prepare what?"

I explained. For some reason he wasn't surprised; he appeared generally indifferent.

"Okay. I'll wait for you at ten o'clock."

"Vadik, I'm begging you, let the children go, please. You

have enough hostages. And it'll make it easier for me to talk to them."

"I was just going to suggest that myself. You can take them. But before you do, you should go and warn your people outside. If they see more than one person leaving, they might decide that we're going to attack the Kremlin."

He agreed so readily to release the children because he'd already planned everything without me; it was important for him to hear that my plan wouldn't change anything. And one more thing: I truly believed that we all had a chance of getting out of this situation. But Vadik knew that wasn't true—for everyone.

The children were taken out one by one. I waited outside, taking each of them by the hand and walking them to the checkpoint. The parents must have been so scared, I thought, that they didn't make a sound when their children were taken away. They couldn't have known for sure where they were going.

Well, "I thought" is an overstatement. I wasn't thinking about anything, except trying not to trip. "Okay, come with me, don't be scared. There's nothing to be afraid of. These are our people . . . Everything'll be okay. Everything is already okay!" Why was I so afraid of tripping? For some reason I thought, if I fall down, I won't be able to get up again.

At the checkpoint, special forces picked the children up and carried them further away. "Easy," I said, "Be careful. These kids have been through enough, and you're carting them around like a sack of potatoes." "Okay, we'll be gentler with them," the soldiers said. "It's just that we're on edge too." Fuck, what kind of life is this?

That was it, the last kid, number twelve.

"Why? Why did they suddenly release the children?" the man in the suit kept asking. It looked like he was from the FSB and the lead person at headquarters.

"I don't know. I asked, and they said, 'Okay, take them.'"

"No conditions? They didn't demand anything—money, vodka, drugs?"

"No, they didn't mention any of that. Vadik, I mean, their

leader, said that I should come back in the morning, at ten o'clock. He wasn't ready to talk to me alone right now."

"He's not ready. Why are they so fixated on that second guy? What for?"

"I have no idea."

"Maybe they're just messing with us, dragging this out? But, again, what for?"

"I don't know. Maybe they just want to have a witness?"

"Don't you want to talk to your friend one more time? Maybe he'll change his mind?"

"No, I don't. Maybe you can talk to him?"

"We've tried."

I looked around. They hadn't wasted any time—they'd brought in a bunch of computers and some electronic gadgets. They hadn't neglected their own needs either. There was no food or drink on the desks, but the aroma in the office left little doubt that they'd polished off a couple bottles of vodka while I was at the church. Good for them, I would've done the same. What's the point of just sitting around staring at one another?

"I could really use a drink."

"Sure, I'll find you a clean glass."

"Don't worry about that."

Here it was, a dream come true. I would have preferred cognac as I didn't like vodka all that much—it didn't sit well with me the first time I tried it—but right now anything would be fine.

"Thanks. I'll go now. I'll be back in the morning, probably around nine o'clock. Call me if you need me."

The guy didn't approve: "We can find accommodations for you here."

"I'll stay at home, thanks."

"Actually, it was decided that until this operation is over, no one leaves the site."

"And who decided that?"

"Well, the higher ups."

"I'm not a participant in this operation, I'm a negotiator, so I'll sleep at home, where my own boss is waiting for me, and I wouldn't question her authority if I were you. So, can Semyonov take me, or should I hitch a ride?"

"Wait, I need to consult my boss."

He came back five minutes later, looking somewhat confused, and said: "Semyonov will take you."

Well, that's great, because you can't imagine how tired I am of your operation zone, of Vadik with his stories, of the sobbing and the stench in the church, of waiting endlessly for Zhenya, of the need to think and make decisions, of your stupid, smug faces—especially your stupid, smug faces. Damn you, scumbags! All this is because of you! It's all your fault!

# 1984

I always hated them. Like everyone around me hated them. Everyone, or so I thought. In my junior year at the university, when I discovered that half of the guys in my class alone had chosen to intern with the Komitet—our slang for the KGB—I was shocked. They'd all seemed like decent people, some were even my friends. "What's so strange about it?" they said in response to my surprise. "It's a good job, with a decent salary. In two years, you'll get to take your first trip abroad. And you get on the list for an apartment right away. Anyhow you Muscovites can afford to be choosy, but what choice do we have? Go back to Tambov?"

Well, that's fine. You have your life, and I have mine.

My life did, however, eventually lead me to the KGB, but through a back door. I guess my life didn't have to go that way, but there weren't a lot of choices—your social being, as Marx said, determines everything.

Around 1983, in Yuri Sobolev's art studio, I met some Americans—two guys and a girl. Yuri asked me: "Could you translate while I tell them about my difficult life as a painter under the yoke of totalitarianism? Maybe they'll buy a painting or two, although it's not likely. They don't look like rich Americans." "Of course, I'll translate."

He was right, they didn't buy any paintings, but they turned out to be interesting people.

They came to Moscow from California to do something that any normal Soviet person would consider suspicious if not just stupid. They came to fight for peace. In California, they would visit all the progressive companies, especially in Silicon Valley, which was picking up steam at that time, and ask for grants, which they usually received. They used that money to educate their countrymen, helping them to see the Soviet Union as more than just an Evil Empire. They tried everything possible to bring the two countries, the two systems closer together. They brought student groups from all over the US to the USSR, staged joint theater performances, organized various exhibitions and festivals, symposiums and colloquiums. But their most cherished dream was to organize telebridges so that Russians and Americans could talk to one another in real time. And then, they believed, there would be no nuclear war. Truly, who could kill people they knew?

They were fantastically naïve but sincere in their American dream. During that time, I was occasionally moonlighting as an interpreter at a place that was called the Soviet Peace Committee, although it gave off a very different vibe.

I asked if they wanted me to help with translating. They were happy to accept my offer, as they'd been assigned some idiot who not only didn't know English that well but was always interfering: "Don't go here," "It's forbidden to go there," "Don't speak to those people," "These are the people you're allowed to talk to."

So, I started helping out. First, because it was interesting to me. And second, there was the American girl, Cindy. I should've married her back then and gone the fuck to California. We would've had grandchildren by now, and I would have left all this shit behind!

Six months later I was summoned to the dean's office, where they told me: "Pyotr Vasilyevich wants to talk to you." "Who's he? And what does he want to talk about?" "He'll explain." Pyotr Vasilyevich introduced himself and showed me his badge. My first thought was that he'd try to convince me to work for them after graduation. They tried once before, but I refused. I told them I wasn't worthy of the honor, that I had a drinking problem, which affected my self-discipline, and anyway, I wasn't suitable due to my ethnic origins. "Don't worry," they said. "We don't engage in antisemitism. We evaluate people as professionals." Somehow, I'd managed to get rid of them, but now they were trying again. These are very persistent people.

But this time was different.

"It came to our attention, Pavel, that you've made some very interesting acquaintances," Pyotr Vasilyevich informed me. "Would you like to tell us more about them?"

"By all means, Pyotr Vasilyevich, I'll tell you everything."

In theory, I'd been anticipating this conversation. It's not like every morning I looked in the mirror and asked myself: Are you ready, Pavel, to face the repressive state apparatus? But I'd rehearsed a declaration about my abject loyalty to the system, which I delivered to Pyotr Vasilyevich: "We met by chance. They're good people. And they have friends in high places. I help them in my free time. What's so wrong with that? It's a good cause—fighting for peace."

"Yes, yes, it's a very good cause," Pyotr Vasilyevich nodded. "Don't worry, we don't have a problem with that. We just need to know what's going on. Do you mind if I call you from time to time? . . . Excellent . . . No need, I have your phone number."

I thought it was over. But just in case, I needed to behave more carefully in the future—at least refrain from staying overnight with Cindy at her Intourist hotel.

That was wishful thinking.

Pyotr Vasilyevich called me ten days later. "My bosses want to meet you in person," he informed me. "Could you stop by the office? Tomorrow afternoon, at half past three. It's a blue building behind the KGB headquarters on Lubyanka Square.

We'll leave a pass for you at the entrance. You have a test—so what? This is more important. Do you want me to call your dean?" No, that was the last thing I wanted.

The blue building in the back of the Lubyanka was the KGB office for the city of Moscow and the Moscow region. Pyotr Vasilyevich introduced me to his boss, Fyodor Pavlovich, and left.

Fyodor Pavlovich was straightforward and unsentimental. He outlined my choices right away:

"Here's the deal, you sign this cooperation agreement, or we can't be of any help to you."

"Why would I need your help?"

"Didn't Pyotr Vasilyevich tell you? We have evidence on you, Pavel, for black marketeering. It's not a serious crime, of course, but it's enough to get you kicked you out of university, and then—if not prison, then definitely the army. And your parents will be asked to resign from their positions. They're working on the ideological front, are they not? Of course, black marketeering is not our business—it falls under the authority of the police—but we're always on the lookout and trying to help good people. In return, of course, we expect that those good people will help us too. Mutual cooperation, as they say."

"And what kind of things will you ask me to do, for example?"

Fyodor Pavlovich turned out to be very direct. He looked me over and instantly understood the kind of operations I would be suited for. "Perhaps, for starters, you could drop in at the synagogue. All kinds of people gather there. Go there, listen, then report back to us."

They were right, my being Jewish wasn't an obstacle for them. "Okay, but I'll have to give it some real thought, look deep into my Komsomol consciousness and decide if I'm worthy."

"Never sign anything, under any circumstances, and play

the fool"—was the advice given to me by Lev Emmanuilovich Razgon, who was the first person I approached. He knew those people very well, having spent sixteen years with them, but on the opposite side of the barbed wire fence.

I played the fool and signed nothing. "You know I'm afraid of my own carelessness; I might inadvertently reveal something I shouldn't. Why don't I just help out, without any paperwork involved?" But they wouldn't back down, and once a week I had to go to the blue house, like a second job.

It lasted for about two months, and after that they left me alone. I guess they finally realized I was hopeless. But it scared me so much, it took several years for the fear to dissipate. I didn't know what else they were capable of doing in that organization, but one thing was certain: they were experts at keeping people in a state of fear.

I put that fear definitively behind me in 1988, when Gorbachev announced the policy of *glasnost*, which didn't turn out to be a bed of roses exactly, but at least two flowers sprang up: the independent newspapers *Svetoch* and *Moskovsky Kuryer*. I wrote about my whole ordeal and took the story to *Moskovsky Kuryer*. Not only did they publish it, they also offered me a job.

What happened next is funny.

Soon after my story was published, I was summoned to the office of Georgy Vladimirovich Strakhov, the editor-in-chief, who showed me a letter: "In response to your publication . . . recruitment of civilians . . . never . . . it violates the norms . . . we are hereby asking you to refute the claim." The letter was on KGB letterhead, with an official seal and a signature: Senior Lieutenant Sinelnikov, Department of Public Relations. "Okay, write a reply," Georgy Vladimirovich said. "Something along these lines: I described an individual experience, there was no intent to generalize, it wasn't my intention to darken the reputation of the KGB, and so on."

Georgy Vladimirovich was a man of firm beliefs but shifting moods. The next morning, after a sleepless night, I brought him the response that I'd agonized over and that was in complete accordance with his guidelines. "What?!" he screamed when he reached the paragraph I was especially proud of: The newspaper regrets that this publication was perceived as an attempt to damage the reputation . . . "Who regrets?! Me?! Let them go to hell!"

Eight years later, Sanobar Habittova from the lifestyle section of the newspaper came back from yet another party, walked straight into my office and said:

"Well, you really have friends in high places. Do you know who asked me to say hello to you? The press secretary of Korzhakov, the head of the president's security."

"Well, you or Korzhakov's press secretary must have been either hallucinating or drunk out of your minds."

"No, he really knows you. You started to fight for reforms in the KGB together."

"Me?! For reforms in the KGB?! Are you sick? Wait, what's his last name?"

Wow! It can't be! It was that very same senior lieutenant, the one whose letter caused me to spend a sleepless night writing a useless response. Sinelnikov. He was already a major. No way . . . What goes on in these people's heads? I wonder if he really believes that together, arm in arm, we fought to clean up the KGB, or was he just playing the fool?

I hate them. So many years have passed, but I still hate them.

But why do I hate *them* in particular? Are the other people really any better? What about the rest of us? And what about me?

"We're here, Pavel Vladimirovich."

"Huh? Sorry, I must have dozed off. How long was I asleep?"

"Since we left Nikolskoye. Let's go, I'll walk you home.

Your whole building, inside and out, will be under surveillance tonight, so don't mind the guys patrolling."

I should invite the neighbors over to show off, I thought.

In the elevator, Semyonov suddenly turned toward me: "Pavel Vladimirovich, I saw how you reacted over there, at headquarters."

"How did I react?"

"With hostility. I just want to tell you . . . I'm not following orders now. People aren't all the same. And neither are the security services."

"Got it. I'll be ready at eight. Good night."

Of course, nothing made sense to me. My head was spinning.

I turned my key in the lock.

# 1:20 A.M.

They won't let you do it. Anything else, but not that—they will not p-p-p-permit it."

When Tanya starts stuttering, it means things are bad. Under normal circumstances, only Lenin in his coffin is calmer than Tanya. And when a person stutters in a whisper, it's even scarier.

"Wait, don't panic. I have an idea."

We were whispering in the bathroom after turning on the shower and the sink faucet. I even remember where I'd read about this method of shielding yourself from surveillance—in the memoirs of the poet Yevgeny Yevtushenko. Allegedly, Robert Kennedy used this trick in a New York hotel room to let Yevtushenko know the position of his brother, the president, at the height of the Cuban Missile Crisis. He was probably lying, but who knows. And who knows if they were even listening in on us or not. On the one hand, Tanya was home all evening; she hadn't gone anywhere. On the other hand, we have no idea of how advanced their technology has become.

"At ten in the morning, I'll go back to the church with Vadik. Then I'll step out—as if he made his demands known. I won't tell them anything, but I'll ask for a press conference. Or I'll tell them what he wants, but still demand a press conference. What'll they do to me: arrest me, kill me, eat me? See, when everyone knows their demands, it'll be too late. After that, there will be only two choices: to accept their demands or refuse them. But what complaints could there be against me?" Then another conversation took place: "I don't know, I'm not sure yet, but what the hell . . . what if?"

Their list contained just one demand. As soon as that demand was met, Vadik and his accomplices agreed to immediately release all the hostages. They didn't promise to turn themselves in, but I wasn't thinking about that.

On the paper with the worn edges that Vadik had shown me three hours ago, back in Nikolskoye, the following was written:

> We demand that the President of the Russian Federation give a speech on television and apologize for the two wars—in Chechnya and Ukraine. After that all the hostages will be freed. If he refuses, they will be killed.

"But don't you understand that he'd never say anything like that on television?"

"Then he's a fool! They're just words! Later, when everything is over, he can claim that he was prepared to do anything to save the lives of Russian citizens, but international terrorism and this new union of Zionists and Banderites have shown their true faces."

"Are you serious? Apologize for Chechnya and Ukraine?"

"Just pretend to . . ."

"You mean allow the terrorists to tell him what to do in front of the whole world? Actually, in front of the whole world wouldn't be as bad as is front of his gang. To show everyone that he can be manipulated? He'd sooner jump from the top of Spasskaya Tower."

"That wouldn't be such a bad option. So, what do we do?"

"I don't know."

W ho could have imagined back in, let's say, 1995 what this man would become? Not to mention, who he'd become: the President of Russia. But twenty years ago, there was no other bureaucrat in the city hall of St. Petersburg who was as pleasant to deal with. No matter what problem you might have in St. Petersburg—getting some official paper, reserving a hotel room during the white nights, or setting up an interview with Mayor Sobchak—just call Vladimir Putin and you'd have nothing to worry about. He was responsible, well-organized, friendly, had a good attitude, and was always at his desk. There was, however, one encounter that happened just after we'd met.

For a long time, I couldn't remember the year it happened: 1994 or 1995? I remember that around that time the *Moskovsky Kuryer* had organized a meeting with our readers in St. Petersburg, and I also remember it being January and that Tanya and I had gotten into a huge fight one evening, but back then that was pretty common, so it didn't help me pin down the year. Then suddenly, a clue: I remembered that readers kept asking about the probability of an attack on Dudayev's palace in Grozny, the former headquarters of the Communist Party of the Republic of Chechnya. So, it was before the attack. It was the winter of 1995, definitely.

Mayor Sobchak was out of town, and the vice-mayor, our future president, was acting as the official host—finding a decent hotel for us, making sure our bus came on time, offering the welcoming toast. What is a meeting with readers? Basically, it's a bender with a few events for actual readers sprinkled in. At one of those parties, I found myself at the same table with Putin and our deputy editor-in-chief, Volodya Rabinovich. As a conscientious host, Putin decided to entertain the guests entrusted to his care with polite conversation. He looked us over and then got straight to the point. I was ready to climb the walls out of boredom and ended up getting drunk as a sow—because I'd heard this schtick at least a thousand times before.

Putin began telling us a story—a long, tedious, plodding story about his recent trip to Israel. He informed us that he went with his family, that he loved everything in Israel very much, and that there were such wonderful people in that country. The first year at the Higher School of the KGB, you take a course—Fundamentals of Recruiting: If you see two Jews, start talking about Israel's achievements. I mean, what else could be of interest to those people? Before I got totally drunk, I tried to think of what he'd be talking about if Rabinovich and I were Kazakh? The next morning, I thought, "Okay, so this guy just wanted to be nice to us, well, to the extent he was able," and I forgot about that evening.

## 1:30 A.M.

I know what I need to do right now. Is there anything to eat?"

"It'll be ready in a second. Want some cognac?"

"No, I already had some vodka there. I'm not gonna drink anymore. I have to get up early tomorrow. Who called?"

"It would be better to ask who didn't call. I muted my cell phone. You can check who called later, if you want. Your parents and Misha are okay. I talked to them at least twenty-five times."

"The others can wait."

I was starving. We barely had any breakfast, then I was busy during the day and didn't eat lunch, and in the evening, as soon as we got home, this farce began. But now I couldn't swallow a thing. That smell from the church stayed in my throat and destroyed my appetite. The people in the church probably felt the same. "Okay, I'll have some cognac—at least it'll give me some calories." I drank without eating anything. Tanya sat across from me.

"Stop looking at me that way."

"What way?"

"Like I'm a corpse."

"Don't even say that! I just feel sorry for you."

"Come on, why would you feel sorry for me? I'm not in anybody's way, not Vadik's and not theirs—it's more like the opposite. And if everything ends well, I could become a Hero of the Russian Federation."

"But, Pasha, you're a coward."

Well, this was quite a day—first, you become the hero of a cheap soap opera, totally against your will, then you realize that you've gotten yourself into some deep shit, and before the curtain falls, the love of your life tells you what she really thinks of you. And, as a sidenote, all this took place on an empty stomach.

"Don't get upset. I didn't mean it like that. You're always saying: the brave man isn't the one who doesn't feel afraid—he's just an idiot. The brave man is the coward who overcomes his fear. You're a coward, and that's why you've been trying your whole life to prove it wrong. Isn't that right?"

"I suppose so. But isn't this a bad time to start psychoanalyzing me?"

"I'm sorry."

What's there to be sorry about? I'm not just your run-of-the-mill coward. You can't even imagine how much of a coward I am. I've known this about myself since childhood. I never got into fights. I knew how to avoid the kind of scuffle that might end with a punch in the face. And I always tried to be friends with the biggest badasses at school, not because I enjoyed their company, but so they wouldn't be my enemies if something happened. I wasn't afraid of pain, or blood. I just didn't want to be humiliated. A black eye isn't such a big deal, but if on the top of being punched in the face they call you a shit-eater or, let's say, a kike and mention your mother in that particular context—how can you show your face after that? I don't know. I wanted to kill the scumbag, but I knew nothing would come of it. I'd just imagine it, clenching my fists. Others could live with it, so why not you, Pasha? Was it pride?

Maybe it was pride, or maybe it was something else—what difference does it make? But I've always known that about myself, and that's probably why I was so attracted to the idea that a brave man is not the one who doesn't feel afraid—he's just an idiot.

I've been truly scared, panic-stricken, twice in my life. First, when the guys from the KGB told me: "Sign the papers or you'll have only yourself to blame," and they promised that my parents would lose their jobs. But that sin was redeemed when I went to the *Moskovsky Kuryer* with my story. (I used to call it an article, but that was the first thing the editor explained to me—articles are only in encyclopedias, but here any text is called a story, and don't try to show off, sonny). I had redeemed that sin, or so I decided. And the second time . . .

That year we went to our vacation spot earlier than usual. As a rule, we went during the first days of September, when that location on the lower Volga River—where Kalmykia, the Astrakhan Region, and Kazakhstan meet—becomes totally deserted because all the tourists with school-age children have already left, and it's still too early for the serious fishermen and hunters; that crowd usually comes later, closer to October.

There were ten or twelve people in our group that would go every year at the very beginning of fall to our favorite place, but that year everyone was desperate to go earlier, as if we'd all caught the same bug: "There's no way we can wait until September, let's go now—we can survive for a week while all the tourists are still there; it won't be so bad. But I just can't stay in Moscow any longer." We went, set up our tents, made our first soup from the fish we caught near the riverbank, smoked our first joint from the local weed, which was the best in the world, and fell asleep. We woke up in paradise: warmth, quiet, sunshine, the smell of autumn on the steppe, and with two weeks of complete happiness lying before us.

But it didn't last long; it ended the moment someone turned on the car radio to listen to the news. What the . . . ? What's the GKChP? . . . trying to save the country . . . Gorbachev could not be located . . . Basically, that was it: On August 19,

1991, all our hopes were dashed. And was it only *our* hopes? What would happen to all of us? To me, for example? Just six months earlier, I'd gotten a job at *Moskovsky Kuryer*, the leading voice of perestroika, RIP . . .

Obviously, our vacation was ruined, but no one knew what to do next. So, we just sat around listening to the news. Wow! Yeltsin climbed on top of a tank and told the GKChP to go to hell . . . people are building barricades on the Krasnopresnenskaya Embankment . . . Will there be an attack? Will there not be an attack? What's happening in other places? And we stood on the bank of the Koksmen River, where it separates from the Volga, with fifteen hundred kilometers between us and the events, and two ferries between us and the nearest phone. We waited. The people have built barricades, the GKChP is issuing orders, Yeltsin is cursing them, but there hasn't been an attack . . .

Should we go back to Moscow? Should we not? On the one hand, all my friends were in Moscow, near the parliament building. On the other hand, I could go, but there would be no friends and no parliament building, only certain comrades waiting for me at my official address.

I was surrounded by a cross section of Russian society. Sergey Voronin began by recalling the fact that he hadn't thrown away his Party card when everyone else in his department, along with the entire university, was doing so, and that his dues were paid up through March. And then he said to me in a patronizing tone: "If something happens, come and see me. I can always find you a position as a laboratory assistant." Andrey Zimin looked at him grimly and said: "Don't go to him for help—he'd be the first to turn you in, and then later he'd explain: 'Well, what could I have done, it's his own fault—he hasn't paid his Party dues since last year.'" Kostya Parfyonov, who only three months before had become an assistant to the newly elected mayor of Moscow, Gavriil Popov, heard the news about special forces invading city hall and whispered in horror: "I told them, when they were planning the remodeling, don't put in parquet floors, use linoleum instead." All the women had turned pale, sensing war, so it was good they found something to do: They all went over to comfort Irina, whose brother was a police captain in St. Petersburg; crowds were gathering there, too.

We sat around like that for three more days, until the GKChP was gone with the wind. We celebrated. Twice, we made Voronin take the ferries to get us vodka: "Go, go, move your ass, collaborator, or we'll tell everyone where your Party card is hidden." Kostya was the first to come to his senses: "That's it, it's time for me to go, I need to get to Moscow right away." "Why the hurry all of a sudden?" "They'll start divvying up state property," Kostya explained, as straightforward as ever. "You don't want to be late for that." The others followed his lead; they also had business to attend to, but I stayed. What's the rush? What's done is done, and my next vacation is a year away.

And so, for many years since, whenever anything bad happens—not some everyday problem, but a serious life-altering misfortune—and I ask myself in frustration, why is all this happening to me, what did I do to deserve this fucked-up country, I relive that summer. I think of the stupor that came over me and the fact that I didn't rush back to Moscow but chose to wait and see how things would turn out. Was I being punished for that? No, I don't believe in mysticism, but if it's not for that, then I totally don't understand you, Lord, not to mention the fact that I don't believe in you. That is, I believe, but not like everyone else.

"You're not forgiven. Is there anything else to drink, or is that all we have?"

"I think you should stop for now."

That was true. Getting drunk in this situation would be . . . too much. It would be the pinnacle of disgrace, as the head of human resources at my first job used to say.

"I've stopped. Okay, if you don't have any other bright ideas, go to sleep. I have something to finish here"

"What is it?"

"You'll find out later, I promise."

"No, seriously, what is it?"

"Could you lay off, please, and do as I ask?" She suddenly burst into tears.

"Lay off?! I'm going nuts here, I've taken all our valo-cardin, and you tell me to lay off! Do you have any idea? You're such an asshole!"

As always, I see myself as a future Hero of the Russian Federation, but in reality, I'm just an everyday asshole.

"Oh, come on, stop it, really. You know, I'm just exhausted. Wait, give me a hug . . . that's right . . . I love you, too."

"So, you won't tell me what you're going to do?"

"I want to write something."

"A will?"

"No, you fool! A story."

For some reason Tanya wasn't surprised. She immediately calmed down, kissed me, and left. She got tired, I guess.

It took me only an hour and a half, which isn't surprising given how many times I'd said all this to myself, and before that I'd rehearsed it among friends. But then I stopped—I'd gotten fed up with arguing and fighting, and, anyway, it's impossible to convince anyone of anything.

# THAT'S RIGHT

W e all deserve this. We didn't earn it, but we deserve it. All of it—this president, an arrogant nonentity, and his nitwit vice-president, and all the ministers with their furtive eyes, and those scumbag deputies, and this boorish state, and our otherworldly television, and ourselves bleating from around the corner . . . Everything has happened for a reason, and we deserve all of this.

No, we don't? We don't deserve this? Not us?

We've done everything right, we've built a new Russia—a democracy, with a free-market economy and all that, and we've worked a lot, haven't we? We've worked a lot, and sometimes it's been hard, because work is not always fun; it can be unpleasant at times. But we kept working—and, by right, getting richer. Well, it's not just that we got richer—look how much has been built: houses, roads, all kinds of stadiums . . . people go on vacation in Turkey, and it's already a common thing . . . in any village store you'll find no fewer than five kinds of beer . . . the streets are full of foreign cars . . . look how service has improved . . . and so on . . . But then Putin came and spoiled everything. We were very critical of him, of course, we even went to a protest rally in 2012—or was it in 2011?—but it was all in vain. Time flies so fast, everything gets mixed up.

Vacations in Turkey, beer, foreign cars, customer service—it's all true. We got richer, that was also true. And those who didn't get richer, or got poorer, they were just losers—what can you do, business is tough, that's how the much-coveted capitalist system works—not everyone reaps the same benefits. Of course, we'd never say the words "low-life" and "trash" out loud—that would be in poor taste, but in reality, ladies and gentlemen, if we look more closely at the excessive cognitive dissonance of Russian society and the civilizing experience of the rest of the world . . . And, of course, we are not unsympathetic to the needs of simple people, we'll donate to Dr. Liza and we'll find some change for Chulpan Khamatova too, and when it comes to a shelter for homeless animals, we collected the money ourselves, with our own hands; there was a special charity auction in a really cool place, the Strelka restaurant, our women donated delicious baked goods. Can you imagine, they baked them themselves. Ksenia Sobchack hosted the event.

And the richer we became, the less we talked. I don't mean small talk. We talked a lot about general topics, but things that only recently had seemed so important and fundamental, we didn't talk about at all anymore. Really, what's wrong with you? As soon as we gather around a table you try to talk about all that crap? Give your Putin a rest already, look at our photos instead, how we drove jeeps in South Africa and how much fun it was, and then we'll have some dessert—it's tiramisu today!

And not only did we refrain from calling people lowlifes and trash out loud, we also never called ourselves elite. The intellectual elite, obviously, what else could we be? But if we're going to be brutally honest, is there anyone else in this country who can claim the title? Of course not. It's just that our inherent delicacy has always demanded excessive modesty. Noblesse oblige, as they say. And when it comes to that other elite, which wasn't shy about calling itself by that name, we were the ones who came up with the joke: elite is an agricultural term, used in modern Russia as a self-signifier by those who have made their fortunes by stealing. We'd come up with all kinds of funny things by that time.

And then suddenly the jokes stopped. Everything got serious.

*When did it happen? When they started killing people in Kyiv? Or when Crimea was occupied? Or Donbas? Or even earlier? When Khodorkovsky was arrested? Or when NTV was closed? What, even earlier than that? When was it? The second Chechen War? The first one? The 1996 elections? If we keep going, we'll soon reach October 1917.*

*And is it true that we have no one to blame but ourselves? Our reaction has always been ethically blameless. Weren't we the ones who never tired of referencing that German Pope whose name I always forget, the one who kept quiet about sexual abuse until his own ass got groped? And we quoted Hemingway too— about fascism being a lie told by bandits, and about the Blackshirts that always come after a reign of mediocrities, just as the Strugatsky Brothers predicted . . . Weren't we the ones? And those renegades who used Brodsky for their own purposes and compared bloodsuckers to thieves for the benefit of the latter— we were the ones who always corrected them, right?*

*So, what didn't work out here? Where is our new Russia, our democracy, and our free-market economy now? And who is to blame? Are the Russian people stupid? Or are the Chekists that devious?*

*Or are there other explanations?*

*Maybe we should remember those who, in 2000, crinkled their noses in disgust, gravely pointing out that Gusinsky hadn't paid his debts, and that's why NTV was punished?*

*Or remember all those people who in 2003 were willing to tell the whole truth about the unsavory methods used by Khodorkovsky to build Yukos Oil. And how many of those knew the situation from the inside?*

*And the hit song "Crimea Can Only Be Russian"—who sang that, do you remember? It wasn't Valeria or Nadezhda Babkina, it wasn't even Joseph Kabzon . . .*

*What are you saying? They closed the* Moskovsky Kuryer? *That's so sad, there was so much good associated with that newspaper . . . but just between you and me,* entre nous, *that publication was so old-fashioned, the media market was reject-ing it . . .*

*Yes, of course, Nikita Mikhalkov, what can you say, it's scary to see what he's become, but that fund of his is harmless—he's helping veterans of the motion picture industry and the the-ater—it would be okay to cooperate with the fund, there's noth-ing shameful in that, and the opportunities it offers . . .*

*No one, of course, would deny that Alexei Navalny does everything right, but those führer-like tendencies of his, and all those rallies, the masses, I've never liked crowds.*

*And you must admit, Yegeniya Chirikova's voice is so-o-o grating, yes, the one who fights to save the forests, and I don't mind, but yesterday it took me three hours to get downtown on the Leningradskoye highway. I was almost late for my manicure. It's terrible, but we still need roads.*

*Over the last fifteen years, who hasn't turned away upon hearing the word "Chechnya" and that all of today's troubles originated there? Who was it who answered with disgust "Well, that's a bit too much," upon hearing the argument that there's absolutely no difference between what happened in Chechnya and the Holocaust? Wasn't that you? Of course, not—you're educated people. You understand everything, you're familiar with universal suffering, and you see through the con artists and thieves—whom you might describe more vividly, given your mastery of the Russian language. But what can you do when there's no one else; so you have to tolerate them because the only way to get by is by partaking of their largesse. And, anyway, we suffered so much under the Soviets, and life is so short.*

*So, you think the Russian people are bad because they don't mourn the loss of civil liberties and don't rally to their defense? But when they were scrounging for crumbs in their factory towns while you were shopping for houses in Chernogoria, were they good then? Of course, you were buying those houses with your hard-earned money—no one is arguing with that. And I'm not even talking about those who weren't just shopping around but were already buying properties, and not in Chernogoria but in Provence. And how did you earn all that money? Honestly, they replied. And when the corpses from Chechnya were transported by the ton and piled up in the city morgue of Rostov, wasn't it you who tried to convince the people that all this was, of course, terrible, but Yeltsyn had no alternative because the cannibal Zyuganov was lurking behind him like a menacing shadow. Were you really concerned about civil liberties back then? Or were you worried about your houses in Chernogoria? Oh, you say that you've been criticizing Putin? But for what? For what he did that Yeltsin didn't do? Start a war? But what about Yeltsyn, the hero of your dreams? Or did you vote for someone else in 1996? Maybe, it's time to answer for this whole mess? Or is revisiting the distant past not* comme il faut*?*

*A hundred people gathered on Pushkin Square in Moscow when the second war in Chechnya began and Grozny was completely leveled to the ground. Only one hundred! Maybe we can add another hundred-fifty old people who wanted to be at the square but were too weak to go. They're the only ones who have the right to blame the Russian people—the others don't. Even those who came to their senses later and went to rally against the war in Ukraine—they don't have the right either, as you should've thought of it earlier if you truly belong to the intellectual elite and aren't some low-life piece of trash.*

*Should I go on? I don't want to. First, it's boring because it's pointless. Second, it's too long—this song could go on practically forever. But what is this song about? It's about the fact that there's nothing unjust, that everyone gets what they deserve, and if it seems you don't deserve this or that, just think a little harder about why you do.*

*And there is no "we"—you should forget this salvatory plural pronoun. Everyone will get what he deserves personally, not* collectively, and, incidentally, a crime committed by a group is punished more severely, as everyone knows. And there is no intelligentsia in the world, it's all a fantasy of Soviet theoreticians. There are intelligent individuals, but a community . . . sorry, but no. Because if it did exist, the history of the last thirty years in Russia could be described in the following way: The staff of a whore house decided to establish self-government within their institution and implement a mechanism for electing their madam, but they couldn't agree on how to divide the profits from this new form of business, and after some hesitation, the bandits, who were protecting the brothel, got the situation under control.

Well, I'm not going to answer for someone else's fuckery. I have enough sins of my own.

## 5:30 A.M.

I t's good."
Startled, I looked up. Shoot, it's already half past five. I'd just put my head down on the desk for a second and three hours went by. Tanya finished reading the text over my head, and I didn't even notice.

"Do you like it?"

"A little too dramatic for my taste, but it's not bad. And I'd get rid of the cursing."

"You can do that yourself when you're preparing it for publication."

"Where are you going to publish it? In *Rossiiskaya Gazeta*?"

"I have no idea. And anyway, that's not my job—my only task here is to write . . ."

A pause. My joke wasn't coming off.

"Honestly, what's come over you?"

"I wasn't sleepy. And let Misha read it, he might find it useful when the next perestroika comes around. No, don't start . . . this is no testament, it's just run-of-the-mill vanity. Now everyone will be asking—who is this Pavel Volodin, what kind of journalist is he? Why haven't we read anything from him for such a long time? And, suddenly, we throw this text in their faces. It'll be a blog on *Ekho*, or we'll place it somewhere better, a feature in *The New Yorker*. And everyone will say in unison: What a brilliant writer, what a sense of civic responsibility, he's as good as Latynina!"

To tell you the truth, it was Vadik who provoked me with his stories.

Here are some other things Vadik told me while we were drinking tea in the church.

Back in 1999, when Basayev decided to move ahead with his campaign in Dagestan and it became clear there would be a new war, Ruslan Sultygov gathered the entire *teip* at his place in Makhkety—well, not the entire *teip*, of course, but the elders and the dignitaries. They spent two days talking and deciding what to do under the current circumstances: whom to support and with whom to fight.

Vadik, obviously, wasn't allowed in, but they let him know the results of their discussion. This is what was decided:

There are many large and powerful *teips*—the *benoy*, *cheberloy*, and *sharoy*—but we are not one of them, there are not so many of us. That's why we won't oppose Maskhadov, but we won't quarrel with Basayev either. Self-preservation is most important for us, but if there is a war, it's clear that we won't just stand on the sidelines. We'll provide people, money, and weaponry, as much as needed, for this national struggle, but don't try to pull us into your unions and alliances, into your politics.

After that, ten men from Makhkety went with Basayev to Chabanmakhi and Karamakhi, and another fifteen joined Maskhadov's militia.

Two days after everyone had left, Ruslan invited Vadik for a talk. "I have a favor to ask," he said. It wasn't often that someone asked a favor of Vadik. "No," Ruslan clarified, "I'm not going to force you to do it, but if you were to agree, I'd be grateful."

"What do you need?"

"It's not, actually, a big deal—there's just a shipment we need to have delivered. Can you drive a pickup truck?"

"Yes, of course."

"Is your driver's license in order?" Vadik had a driver's license, he got it back in bootcamp, it's just that no one had ever asked him about it. "And it's not really my shipment, but some important people asked me," Ruslan told him. "You see, the war will start any day now, but business is the kind of thing that has to go on no matter what, trade must continue, goods have to move, and money has to change hands, regardless of whether there's a war. In short, there's one shipment left at Karachay's warehouse, and we need to deliver it to Russia. We have everything, a truck with Rostov license plates, official papers, an invoice, money for the trip, but we don't have a driver. If we put someone local behind the wheel, it would create even more problems. He'd be asked to pay a bribe at every checkpoint; they might even take the shipment and seize the truck—it's totally lawless out there. How would that make our respectable businessmen look in front of their partners? But with your appearance and your last name, you shouldn't have any problems with the delivery. And don't worry, you aren't on the most wanted list, we took care of that—you were at one point, but not anymore. After you deliver the shipment, come back and live with us. It would be good to get you married. It's too bad you're not a Chechen, although you are Muslim. Though, there is a widow who's been asking about you. But we'll deal with that when you get back. So, will you do it?"

Vadik didn't ask who these respectable people were that wanted to save face in front of counteragents in Russia—unnecessary questions only create more problems. About three days before the *teip* meeting, Basayev came and talked with Ruslan for an hour and a half. Everyone knew that he had some dealings with Russia, but no one really looked down on him for that—you need to support your regiment somehow. Maybe Basayev had asked? "Nonsense," Vadik decided. "Who am I compared to Shamil? Anyway, it's none of my business. If they asked, that means it's necessary. I'll do it."

He was stopped just once, at the checkpoint in the village of Privolny, where two state roads merge and where they stop everyone without exception. "What are you carrying?" they asked, barely checking his driver's license and registration. "Seventy bags of sugar, here's the invoice, and here's the itinerary." "Okay, there are two options: we can put you in the line for inspection—as you can see from here, the entire area is full, it would take about four hours—or we can speed up the process." Vadik paid, as Ruslan instructed him, and kept on driving. He arrived at his destination without any misadventures, parked his truck at some warehouse on the outskirts of the city of Volgodonsk, unloaded the cargo, noticed that no one asked for any papers, and then began his journey back, happy that he hadn't let his people down.

One month later, in September, when Vadik was watching TV and saw an explosion in an apartment building, corpses without heads, and people screaming in horror, he couldn't help thinking . . . but he didn't really need to think. He realized instantly and without a doubt what he had brought to that city and why. He didn't need any proof, plus who would he even ask? Ruslan? Or, God forbid, Basayev? He understood everything. When the same happened in Buynaksk, and then in Moscow itself, Vadik didn't spend an extra minute in front of the TV—hadn't he seen enough corpses? The situation was crystal clear—he had very little time to get away. Anyone who so much as stood in the vicinity of such acts, even unknowingly, even if they'd been used as blind mules, winds up dead.

Now, while there was war and chaos, he still had a chance to escape, but it wouldn't be there for long.

He was sorry to leave the widow, Khadizhat. Ruslan didn't know, but they'd gotten together even before Vadik's trip to Volgodonsk. They hit it off straight away, and everything was going so well between them that Khadizhat even went to talk to her clan's elder—of course, she couldn't hope for a wedding as he wasn't Chechen, but at least they could arrange for him to live in her house so she wouldn't get any more dirty looks. Otherwise, what kind of love was it—a roll in the hay? Later, Vadik longed to find out what had happened with Khadizhat, but how?

That would have to wait—now he had to run. Which was what Vadik had been doing for most of his adult life.

It was already the winter of 2000. The Russian army had already crossed the Terek River and advanced deep into Chechnya, Kadyrov Senior had already abandoned the town of Argun, Grozny had been shelled, and columns of refugees were walking toward the Georgian border. Vadik took all his savings from his secret hiding place, grabbed some warm clothes and left during the night. He walked to the freeway leading to Itum-Kale and asked for a ride in the back of a truck loaded with old furniture. He went without saying goodbye— not to Khadizhat, let alone Ruslan. It was better to stay alive.

In three days, he'd crossed the border at Pankisi Gorge. There were three villages inhabited by local Chechens, and that winter, they'd formed a camp behind enemy lines consisting of refugees, the injured, soldiers in need of rest, and those who were preparing to replace them near Grozny and in Komsomolsky. From time to time, Maskhadov, Gelayev, and Barayev would also come to take a break from the action. There was no trace of any Georgian authorities, no one asked for any documents, and you could stay there for a while—to get some rest and look around. But he understood that such happiness wouldn't last very long, let alone forever.

He didn't know what to do next, but now, finally, he got lucky. A group of about fifteen men came down from the mountains to Pankisi. They looked like Russians, but they had a strange way of speaking, and they definitely weren't locals. Vadik listened, observed, and then approached them. They turned out to be Ukrainians. They'd finished their second deployment in Chechnya through UNA-UNSO, or something like that. Vadik had heard about them before. They were fighting not so much for the Chechens but against Russia, and they were good soldiers. But he'd never had a chance to meet them. Now they were trying to get back home. "And who are you?" they asked Vadik. He told them his story, omitting any unnecessary details, the things he himself would be happy to forget. "Can I come with you?" Vadik asked. "Sure, why not, we need people with experience. Can you swim? We'll have to cross the sea, and if something happens . . . Our cargo, as you can probably guess, is every border patrol's dream."

A week later, a bus arrived, they all got in and drove to the port of Poti, where they boarded a cargo ship and sailed to Odesa. But they never reached Odesa. They switched to two small boats, which they moored in the lagoons, and then they went by foot, occasionally hitching rides, and ended their journey somewhere near the city of Rovno.

"Where are you going now?" Oles, their boss, asked. Vadik shrugged his shoulders. Nowhere. He had nowhere to go.

L et's have some breakfast, otherwise I'll die of starvation, not like an epic hero, and no one will care about my stories."

The smell was gone, just when I thought it would stay with me forever. Oh, Tanya, you're a genius and a hero! Look at all this: fried eggs with tomatoes, and pancakes with jam, and fresh juice, and tea with thyme. Now this is living. If only . . .

"Do you have any idea what you're going to do?"

"Nothing other than what I told you before."

"It's not much . . ."

"Then you come up with some better ideas. We don't have a lot of options. I need to try, then we'll see how it goes."

"And if . . ."

"And if, and if . . . there are so many different ifs . . . Let's look at the bright side. We don't have time to agonize over this. We had to make a decision, and now we have to act on it. And if we don't? Then we're as good as dead. That's it."

"Damn him, damn your Vadik!"

"He's as much yours as he is mine. Tanya, this conversation is useless."

"We're useless . . ."

"True enough . . . We're wasting time. Can I invite the colonel now to have coffee with us?"

"Wait, let me comb my hair."

I have no doubt that, upon hearing the trumpets on judgement day, Tanya will say: "What?! No, I can't, I have an appointment at the hair salon on Pokrovka." And I don't envy the archangels who decide to argue with her.

"Okay, call your colonel."

"Let me introduce you. This is Tatyana."

"Yes, I know. I'm Sergey."

"Would you like some coffee?"

Colonel Semyonov, who turned out to be named Sergey, stumbled:

"Well, actually . . . Yes, I would. Thank you."

Next to my cup I'd put the piece of paper on which I'd copied Vadik's ultimatum. Colonel Sergey didn't bat an eye, just glanced at the text, read it, then looked up.

"Excellent coffee! Did you make it with cinnamon, Tanya?"

Tanya confirmed that yes, she adds some cinnamon and also some cardamom. Enjoying the coffee, the colonel nodded, then took out his cell phone, showed it to us, brought his hand to his ear to indicate that someone was listening, and continued the small talk:

"How unusual, with cardamom . . . it gives the coffee a very interesting taste." At the same time he indicated that he needed a pen. Tanya ran into the other room.

Semyonov wrote down two words, showed me, then folded the paper along with my text and put them in his pocket.

"We should probably go, Pavel Vladimirovich, it's time. Tatyana, thank you very much for the coffee. By the way, if you need anything, don't hesitate for a second, just tell the guys outside, they can do anything—bring you something, take you somewhere, and bring you back, of course. Please, don't take it the wrong way, an order is an order—we need to keep you under surveillance at all times and make sure you have no contact with anyone."

"What is this, house arrest?"

"Just a few restrictions for the duration of the operation."

I could see that Tanya was getting angry. I gave her a look:

Don't, it's not the right time or place, it's not a priority right now.

Sergey Semyonov had the delicacy to leave the flat first, closing the door partially behind him. We hugged each other.

"I memorized it. I won't betray you." That's what he'd written in response to my message about Vadik's demands. I whispered those words in Tanya's ear—well, their meaning, that he wouldn't betray us.

And then I whispered three more words.

In response, she grabbed my ears, put her forehead against mine and said: "I categorically forbid you to urinate." My eyes opened wide, but then I remembered . . .

I have a friend, Petya Kuzmenko. Although his name is Petya Kuzmenko, he's an American, born and bred, not even an immigrant. During WWII, the Nazis sent Petya's mother and father to Germany, where they ended up in the American occupation zone. They later made it to the US, where they met and had their son, Petya. Their ethnic roots were sacred to them, and they spoke only Russian at home—so Petya grew up completely bilingual. He came to Moscow, I think, in 1990 because he decided to personally observe the renovation underway in his beloved historical homeland and Russia's ascent to the pinnacle of progress. To experience life to the fullest, he brought along his young wife, Abby.

Everything was going extremely well. His homeland was indeed remaking itself and on the rise, Petya was freelancing for every existing American publication, Abby was making progress in her study of the Russian language, and they were welcome at the most sophisticated parties in Moscow. But there was one sorrowful note—Abby couldn't get pregnant, and she really wanted to.

"Why don't you go see my friend Palych at the Institute of Obstetrics and Gynecology? It's not American medicine, obviously, but hey, they know a few things too, and here two hundred dollars is big money, so you're not risking anything. It couldn't hurt to try."

That was the best advice I'd ever given to anyone. Two months after their first visit to Palych, Petya and Abby gave a special dinner to celebrate the fact that Abby's period was definitively late, which they announced with their uniquely American directness.

Palych assigned Vasya Gryaznov as Abby's obstetrician, and she had enormous faith in him. Because the ruble was so cheap at the time, Petya could afford to feed the future mother of his child with black caviar just from his royalties. But by the eighth month of Abby's pregnancy, they had to say goodbye to Moscow, the parties, Palych, Vasya, and the cheap caviar. Insurance, citizenship, grandparents, and a host of other issues dictated that they go to New York for the delivery. They gave a farewell party and left.

Two days later, there was a call at four o'clock in the morning. It was Petya from New York. "What happened?" "Well," Petya said, "I came home and found Abby turning blue and shaking. I asked her what was wrong, and she says, 'My doctor forbid me to urinate.' 'What?!' 'Yes, he forbid it.'" "What kind of nonsense is that?" Petya and I asked each other simultaneously. "She's sitting here in front of me, shaking and turning completely blue, imagine that, and absolutely refuses to . . . you know." "Okay, I'll try to figure out what's going on."

It was four o'clock. In the morning. Because of the time difference. But we couldn't wait until morning. Or Abby would die because, as Petya explained, she had unconditional faith in Vasya and wouldn't listen to anyone else.

I was able to reach Palych, who woke up Vasya. Then Palych called me back, and soon the good news was flying over the Atlantic Ocean: The doctor said she could pee!

We learned something else as well. While in New York,

Abby wasn't feeling well—something was throbbing, and she instantly called her doctor, Vasya, whose advice she followed to the letter. It was half past eight in the evening in Moscow. Vasya was celebrating the end of the work week with one of his nurses when Abby called. After listening to Abby's complaints, he gave her some advice. "Abby," he said, eager to get back to his nurse, "in your condition, the most important thing is not to piss yourself," which in idiomatic Russian means 'to stay calm,' 'don't panic,' but Abby's Russian wasn't quite there yet.

I can see why Tanya is reminding me of that story right now. Good for her. Even though we've already pissed ourselves, so to speak.

H oly crap, just look who they've brought here . . . with his shovel-shaped beard for all to see. Forgive me, Father, for I have sinned! Mobilizing him meant they'd really studied my biography to find the ideal person to talk to me. There was Sasha on the porch of the Nikolskoye municipal building; Sasha wearing a cassock and a cross over his chest. His work clothes, as he used to say.

"Greetings, Father Alexander!"

"Hello to you, my son!"

That greeting had been our joke of choice for the past fifteen years, since Sasha was ordained. There was a second part to it: "And, Father, when you die from too much vodka and too many female parishioners, may I say a requiem for you? And if you really are a father to me, will you leave something to your progeny?" But this time I skipped it—it felt like too much today.

Sasha and I had been classmates; we went to the same high school. Were we friends? It's more like we were members of a club for people into heavy metal, excessively flared jeans, and books that were, if not prohibited, then not exactly recommended, like *Master and Margarita*. Our pastime of choice was a kind of hippie wandering between Pushkin Square and Trubnaya Square, and we indulged, not in vulgar port wine, the drink of the proletariat, but in weed, the choice of the elite. Back then it seemed like a real friendship that would last forever. But after graduating from high school, we lost touch pretty quickly and didn't talk for a long time. We met again ten years later, when I was already working at *Moskovsky Kuryer*, and it felt like we were living in a totally different country. At least, that's how it felt back then.

Sasha, as I later learned, graduated from seminary at the Holy Trinity-St. Sergius Monastery. Who would've thought— no one saw that coming—and his father was a vice-rector of the Higher School of the Communist Party to boot. After seminary, he began graduate school and tried to get ordained, but there were always jealous schemers standing in his way. His dream finally came true, but by that time, new and unexpected horizons were opening up. Gorbachev decided to legalize the practice of religion. The thousandth-year anniversary of the baptism of Rus was celebrated as if it were the anniversary of the October Revolution. Before our eyes the Patriarch became an influential and independent figure. Soon, near the Kremlin, the Cathedral of Christ the Savior began to rise up with unprecedented speed. Monasteries and churches were coming back. On Easter, the lines at churches were like the lines to get into hockey games. And on religious holidays, all the higher-ups felt obliged to stand in the front row.

Sasha worked at the patriarchate in the department of public relations, writing speeches for the patriarch, among others. He was assigned to work with all the progressive publications in Moscow to promote the renewed church. His first stop was *Moskovsky Kuryer*, a citadel of progressive ideas, and that's where we met again.

Our friendship was resurrected. Sasha's stories weren't bad, they didn't contradict our editorial policy, he accepted all corrections and cuts without offense, and most importantly, there was no fanaticism in him, just the opposite—he turned out to be funny, cynical and, therefore, an excellent drinking companion. Sasha used to entertain us: "They tell me the Jews crucified Christ. I answer: This may be true, but if the Jews didn't crucify Christ, then wouldn't we be out of work?" All that didn't prevent him in more recent days from writing a major political story—thank God, not for *Moskovsky Kuryer*, which had by then given up the ghost. It was about a global conspiracy against the Russian World, in which non-Russians played a significant role, and about the necessity of unifying around you-know-who in these fateful times. The next time I saw him, it was at the birthday party of the newspaper *Kommersant*, where I asked: "Do you even understand what you're doing?" He answered: "When you did what you wanted, we kept quiet, now it's your turn to watch in envy."

"Okay, go ahead, tell me what they've instructed you to do."

"Drop it. I came here of my own volition."

"I'll drop it when I decide to drop in, not when you tell me to. Of your own volition? What are you going to do of your own volition? Preach to me? Or offer me communion?"

Neither the former, nor the latter, as I found out. And anyway, Sasha hadn't come here to save my soul, as he said. Did he volunteer or did they make him come? I chose not to ask. According to Sasha, he heard the news, called someone—what difference does it make who—told that person that he knew the major participants and offered his services. What services? Even Sasha couldn't explain that, but he felt that he needed to be closer to the events. They allowed him to come to Nikolskoye, told him what had happened and complained about Zhenya, who didn't want to participate in the operation. Sasha went to talk to him, but Zhenya resisted, like a ram before the slaughter. He repeated his schtick about his two or three children, then cursed us all and went back to sleep. He even refused to have a drink.

I wasn't the only one who'd spent the previous night working hard.

They did actually know each other. Whenever Sasha went to Petrovsky monastery on business, he never passed up the opportunity to stop by *Moskovsky Kuryer*, which was just two buildings down, regardless of whether he had a story in an upcoming issue. And why not? They'd always pour him a drink and offer him something to eat; he'd hear the latest rumors, and the women who worked there were good-looking. That's how he met Zhenya. "Actually, you must've seen Vadik too?" "Probably," Sasha acknowledged. "I remember someone with blond hair, but he didn't stand out."

"Okay, it's no big deal about Zhenya, I couldn't convince him either . . . we'll figure it out . . . all that doesn't matter anymore . . . sorry, but I don't have time for you right now."

At this point, he really surprised me. He offered himself instead of Zhenya. "You? You want to go with me to the church to see Vadik?" "Yes." "Don't you realize how they might feel about priests?" "How?" "I didn't ask. But I can imagine. Are you looking for your Golgotha?" Sasha wasn't in search of heroic feats, but he was prepared to go . . .

Sasha's offer took me by surprise, but it was a great relief too. What's the point in lying, it was much better to go with someone, regardless of who that someone was. I didn't expect this from you, Father Alexander, honestly.

"Thanks, Sasha."

"Don't mention it. Wouldn't you go with me if, God forbid, the roles were reversed?"

It was a very flattering assumption, but I wasn't sure. Honestly, if I could have found a reasonable pretext, I would've reconsidered going even now.

"Okay. But I don't think it'll work without some preparation. He insisted on Zhenya coming, so I have no idea how he'll react to you. I'll go and ask, maybe it'll be okay."

"Are you afraid?"

Was everyone going to ask me that question today?

"A little. Aren't you?"

"No, I'm not afraid. I went to the doctor on Thursday. Next week, I begin chemotherapy. They say there's some hope. I'm my doctor's priest, so he wouldn't lie to me. I've been thinking that it might be better to have atheist doctors. So, that's how it is."

That's how it is. I get it. How right that man was who said at his ninety-fourth birthday party: "Life, Pasha, is the gradual disappearance of your enemies." And of your friends, too, of course. But it's easier to make friends, as strange as it may seem. In fact, life has become very strange: you don't know who's a friend and who's an enemy.

"Okay, I'll go and ask Vadik about you. Let's see what he says."

"I'll be here. By the way, have you seen the rector among the hostages?"

"No, but I wasn't really looking for him. Do you want me to ask?"

"Yes, please. I know him. He's a good man. With four children. Good luck."

Good luck to you too.

A t headquarters, everything was the same—the senseless bustle, the stale air, angry and lost faces, which were thoroughly worn out by now.

What's new? I learned that, at four thirty this morning, they released one woman from the church—she had a nosebleed, from high blood pressure, probably. The EMTs treated her in the ambulance; she could talk, but she was of no help to the operation. She hadn't really seen anything, and what she had seen, she didn't remember. She just sobbed and wailed.

That's about all the news that happened while I was away. And what were the higher-ups saying? Well, what priceless advice were we getting from the very top, from somewhere near Staraya Square? Take no prisoners, don't hesitate to use bullets, you sons of bitches . . . ? It's not really in the scope of your duties, they told me. Okay, good, it's not like I really wanted to know. So then, I'll enter a den of terrorists—does that fall within the scope of my duties? They didn't say anything about Sasha's proposal—which meant he'd discussed it only with me. Well, I won't say anything either, for now. Vadik might completely reject the offer, so why put the cart before the horse?

They didn't even say goodbye before I went in.

The soldiers from special forces were different; it seems there'd been a changing of the guard. "It's just you and me now, Colonel—the only veterans of this operation." Semyonov didn't answer; he just nodded, without even turning his head in my direction.

## 10:12 A.M.

There was some activity in the church as well. I couldn't see anything from the door, but I could hear voices giving commands, and footsteps—something was being moved from one place to another. Vadik didn't let me go any further. We talked in the same storage room where yesterday he'd told me about all his adventures over the many years we hadn't seen each other. But he hadn't told me everything, as I soon found out.

# THE 2000S

Oles took a liking to Vadik. "If you want," he said, "I can find a job for you. They won't pay you, but they'll provide room and board, I promise you that, plus, there are no cops around. You have a Russian passport? Don't worry, even a Chinese one would be fine. Your job? Well, it's not the uranium mines. Plus, do you really have a lot of other options?"

A week later Vadik found himself in the hamlet of Buyan. It was fourteen kilometers to the nearest village and a good eighty to the regional center. The hamlet was surrounded by woods, there was the Strombylikha River, and on a clear day, you could see the Carpathian Mountains. No one else lived nearby. It used to be a hunting farm, with two solid houses, a stable, a bathhouse, and various sheds. Later the hunting farm was sold, along with the compound. Who became the owner of those houses and that huge piece of land? God only knows. The people who lived in Buyan and took care of the place might have known the new owners, but they were in no hurry to share that information with Vadik.

They were a family of four. A father and a mother, Alexey Grigorievich and Tamara Illarionovna, and two grownup sons, Andry and Yuri. During school breaks, Yuri's daughters, Anka and Liza, would come to stay. There were no other visitors if, of course, you don't count the young men, who were the main reason this hamlet continued to exist. They used to come every other week, in groups of ten to fifteen; the former stable couldn't accommodate more—and they'd usually stay for about three days.

Vadik didn't need to be told what those guys were doing in Buyan, going into the woods in the morning and only coming back in the evening or at night. He figured it out from overheard snippets of conversation. Those conversations were in Ukrainian, but Vadik learned the language pretty quickly, plus, some words sound the same in Russian. Daytime and nighttime marches, hand-to-hand combat, assembling and disassembling of rifles, and land navigation—these guys were undergoing basic military training. And they weren't being forced or bullied into it, as Vadik was in bootcamp. It was obvious they wanted to do this.

There was a lot to do in Buyan, but Vadik's work wasn't difficult or unfamiliar. Feeding the cow, cleaning up after her, tossing the hay, chopping wood, protecting the vegetable garden—in short, the same things he did in Makhkety, but the land was better here and there was more of it, about three hectares. He tried not to think about Makhkety and his previous life.

The family took their time getting to know Vadik. A year and a half after Oles brought him to Buyan, Alexey Grigoriyevich asked Vadik to stay after supper for the first time. He offered him a shot of *samogon* and started asking questions. Vadik answered truthfully; the only thing he left out was his trip to Volgodonsk. Why did you leave Chechnya? The war started again, and when the federal troops come, or a new government is set up, won't I be first one arrested? Tamara Illarionovna asked about his mother. Vadik's answer was short, but there wasn't enough for a long story anyway. "Married?" "I was." "Any children? Did you get divorced?" "No, we didn't, there wasn't enough time. That's how it all happened." "I see. Another shot? Have you heard about the Golodomor? Do you know what country used to be in this region? No, earlier than that, before the war. No, not the Chechen war, but the sense-less one, the Great War . . ."

The men in the family treated Vadik alright, but the mother, Tamara Illarionovna, felt truly sorry for him, and when Yuri hit Vadik in the heat of the moment for having allowed the new hay to get wet, she scolded her son and slapped him hard. Holding his throbbing ear, Yuri said: "That's it, Vadik, you really live here now. She wouldn't get so angry about a stranger."

When they were in Buyan, Anka and Liza liked to talk to Vadik. In their boarding school, everyone spoke in Ukrainian; they studied Russian as a foreign language. The girls wanted some practice, and, besides, they thought the way Vadik spoke Ukrainian was very funny.

Suddenly, in the winter of 2004, the guys, or the cadets as Vadik called them, stopped coming. Listening to the conversations at the dinner table, he was able to figure out why. And later, watching the news reports from Kyiv of protesters gathering for the first Maidan uprising, he saw a few familiar faces—guys who'd trained at Buyan.

"Vadik, do you understand what's going on?" Alexey Grigoriyevich asked him. Vadik looked him straight in the eye and said: "Don't take me for a fool. I understand everything."

The fools, it became clear, were those who'd thought Vadik was good-natured but brainless, and because of that, quiet. Like I did, for example.

I'm sorry to interrupt. They're waiting for me at headquarters to tell them the news."

"That's okay, they can wait. I want you to hear my story to the end and understand it."

His speech became different somehow—dry, almost hostile, and he stopped calling me Uncle Pasha.

"Okay. But someone else has arrived here. You might remember him. He was a frequent guest on Petrovka Street—Sasha Kurlin, the priest."

"I remember."

"He's offered to replace Zhenya."

"Why all of a sudden? Is he planning his ascension?"

"I don't know. But you wanted a second person."

"Not anymore. There's no need. Remember the response to the password in the film *The Elusive Avengers*? 'He was needed, but not anymore.' Just like now."

T en years—is it a lot or a little? It depends on where you are. In prison, it's probably a lot. In a happy marriage, it's too little.

Life was going well for Vadik in Buyan. Because his life was simple. Room and board, work that wasn't hard—he had it all. And the people around him weren't mean. There was no need to rush off. There was no need to kill anyone. And no one needed him—meaning, no one wanted to take his life. He'd even started to reminisce. First, it was good memories: the utility closet at our editorial office on Petrovka Street, the first place of his own he'd ever had. It wasn't a bunk bed in a communal barracks, it wasn't the barn in Makhkety, but a private space he'd never known before. He recalled how Nina taught him to kiss, and how he agonized over it, thinking all that experience must make her a slut. And he recalled the moment he realized that he would definitely kill the sergeant, even if it meant prison—that was good too; he felt such relief after making up his mind.

Everything else came back too, all of Vadik's life. But he wasn't afraid of it anymore. It first took Vadik by surprise, but it was a fact—his fear was gone. He was able to remember, to think and do nothing, just think. And then fall asleep.

Ten years isn't nothing. But it's not a lot either. It depends on what happened before.

But then 2014 came. And everything broke down again. Such is fate.

Everything definitively collapsed after Anka got injured. It was as if Tamara Illarionovna had foreseen it—whenever she could tear herself away from the TV, she would pray that Anka not go there: "It's not a woman's job, let the men fight that son of a bitch, she's just a girl." By that time, Liza had already gotten married and left for Canada with her husband. Anka went to Kyiv to go to medical school. She didn't get in on her first try, so she started working as a nurse's assistant in a neurology department.

When the protests started, Anka put on some warm clothes, drew a red cross on herself, took all the painkillers the head physician could get for her, and went to the Mikhailovsky Cathedral, where the injured were being taken—they were afraid that the police would arrest them in the hospital. When all hell broke loose in the vicinity of Institutskaya Street, it was near the very end—one day later, Yanukovich would flee, and it would all be over in Kyiv. Anka ran to the barricades near the Arsenalnaya metro station; she'd been there before and thought it was safe. But now there were snipers, and one of them shot Anka. The red cross hadn't protected her. It was a very serious wound: the bullet entered between her seventh and eighth vertebrae. She would live, but what kind of life would she have, in a wheelchair at the age of twenty? Well, it is what it is. They were thankful she was alive.

Tamara Illarionovna couldn't get up for three days after learning about Anka. Then she came to and started packing— she'd go to the city, forever. How could they live here with a handicapped child when even the toilet was outside? Yuri and Andrey had already left, to go to the Maidan. Vadik never saw them again. He helped Alexey Grigoriyevich with the final arrangements—removing anything of value, taking the cow to the market to sell, closing the shutters, and Godspeed.

No one needed that farm anymore; its time was over. Fighters would now be trained in different places.

At least that's what the guy who came to see Vadik told him. He'd been sent by Oles, who by that time had become an important person. He'd stopped coming to the farm, but he hadn't forgotten Vadik.

"Will you go with us?"

"Where? What for?" This is what they needed Vadik for: During the fighting near Ilobaiskoye, they intercepted conversations that were taking place in a language no one could understand; but it didn't take long to figure out it was Chechen. Kadyrov had brought his people. Their base was near Gorlovka—which was in their zone of responsibility. "You understand Chechen, right?" Vadik had never learned how to speak the language—the pronunciation was too difficult for him. "Understand? Yeah, a little." "There's not a lot you need to understand anyway, just when, where, how many people, what military equipment, are there any dead or wounded. Well, what do you say? Excellent, pack your bags."

For a long time, Vadik was unable to figure out why he'd said *yes* to this offer. What, he hadn't had enough wars in his life? Quite the opposite. Was there no place for him to go? That wasn't it. He knew that wherever he ended up, he'd survive. Was he afraid that if he refused, they'd send him back to Russia? He wasn't afraid anymore. It's not that he'd forgotten how to feel fear, something had just gone numb inside.

It turned out to be worse than Chechnya. Everything seemed the same, only worse. Back in Chechnya, it wasn't so ruthless. At least occasionally, someone would spare someone else's life. While they didn't take any prisoners among the contractors or special forces soldiers, they never killed recruits, unless it was absolutely necessary. And our side didn't execute people without an order, unless someone had completely lost their mind. It wasn't like that here. Who was fighting whom? Who was the attacker, and who was the defender? The answers changed from day to day, and that drove everyone crazy . . .

Vadik got lucky again, sort of. He ended up in a battalion where there were no recruits, only volunteers, and the youngest was twenty-four years old. They knew how to fight, didn't go berserk on the third day of combat, and even tried to observe some kind of discipline . . . How they carried that out, well, that's another story. They arrested two soldiers for assaulting a girl from the orphanage for developmentally disabled children in Torez—no one had bothered to evacuate those children. The orphanage continued to function, but they didn't have any food left. So those two soldiers got a loaf of bread and some candy and went over to the orphanage. Later, they were stupid enough to brag about the good time they'd had, and rumors started to spread. They tied the two men's hands and feet, put balaclavas over their heads, then lowered their pants and left them outside overnight. The mosquitos in July are like crocodiles over there, so within two hours they'd started screaming so loudly, it was impossible to sleep. The commander took pity and ordered them to be executed.

"Then why did you agree? You could've said no. And why didn't you run away? You must've had the chance. But most importantly . . . what happened next? I mean, why are we here?"

"You fucked me over."

This was so unexpected, it startled me. There was one thing Vadik never allowed himself to do in front of us—curse.

"Who?"

"You. You've fucked everyone over. You're scumbugs who torture people."

"You . . . Who's the *you* here?"

"Russians"

It was an interesting plot twist. I'd come across something like this once before.

It was in December 1994, when we were electing the first

Duma—even the name was brand-new back then. I went to the polling station, cast my vote, and left—there were no exit-polls yet, the discipline of sociology was just being rehabilitated. So, I thought I'd conduct my own poll and went to the nearest body shop to chat with the mechanics and get a feel for what the people thought about the present moment. A body shop was just the right place for such a poll—you can find all social classes there, from plumbers to academics.

And there truly was the full social spectrum at that body shop. Everyone was standing around a nice spread on the hood of a car, and some people were already completely drunk, having probably been there for a while. 'Oh, look who's here!" "Come over here!" "Pour him a shot!"

Naturally, the conversation was about the election—who voted for whom, who was against whom, who among the candidates was a jerk, and who wasn't. But the number of interlocutors was rapidly decreasing. They'd been there for some time drinking and were now dozing against the wall.

Very soon there were only two of us left standing—me and Kolya, nicknamed Samodelkin—Mr. Do-It-Yourself. The rest were napping. So, we're standing there smoking when Kolya says, thoughtfully:

"To be honest, you should've executed the Communists back then, in '91."

"Wow, that's some idea . . . whether to wipe out the communists is a topic for discussion. But who do you have in mind? Who should carry it out?"

"C'mon, you know me, I'm not that way, and neither are the guys . . . but you're a Jew."

"Great! So, you're saying it's the Jews who should kill the communists? While you put your feet up?"

Formulating the question in this way greatly puzzled Kolya. But he gathered his wits, thought for a while, and came up with the answer. He looked around at the bodies sleeping along the wall, bodies that looked more like giant amoebas than human beings, and said reproachfully:

"Look at them. Do you seriously believe they're capable of accomplishing anything?"

And now, here was Vadik with his ethnic theories . . . which, we should duly note, he'd put into practice.

He was acting on his own. No one had coached him, he hadn't consulted anyone, and he didn't expect any help. By that fall, only remnants remained of his battalion—some had been killed, others, injured. Vadik survived only because he was sitting at headquarters and not in the trenches wearing headphones. New people were coming, youngsters mostly, many were locals. Vadik examined them and made his selection . . . He took only orphans, those whose parents had died in Kyiv during the protests or here, when cities and villages were passed among the warring parties with each liberator cleansing the territory. He had no trouble finding recruits. He recruited people who were desperate, but not insane. Weapons, explosives, bullets—there was no shortage of them either. Video cameras and laptops were easy to get. There were plenty of stores around that had yet to be completely ransacked. The most difficult thing was finding a spot where you could connect to the Internet, but they had a guy who knew about that stuff.

Over a single nighttime march, they passed through the battle zone and crossed into Karacharov, where the border was like a sieve. They found an abandoned village on the other side and settled in. They had plenty of money, but Vadik didn't say how they got it. At the market in Taganrog, he bought a minibus, came back for his crew, and in a single day they made it to Nikolskoye along the new highway, named The Don, after the river. It was fast and had very few checkpoints, but of course, getting through them wasn't cheap. They didn't attack the church right away—they took a month to prepare. They got lucky: the rector had gotten some money from the diocese, and the parishioners had collected some too, for renovations: to fix the floors, replace a beam and check the wiring, along with some minor repairs that had piled up over the years. But the amount of money they could offer was so laughable that even Tadzhiks refused to do the work. But Vadik's crew accepted, saying they were refugees and in dire need of earning some money. They lived in a shack near the church.

Well, and now we're here . . .

"Did I fuck you over, too?"

"Have you checked your passport recently? Do you still live here, or have you emigrated?"

"No, I still live here. There's no way you would have found me if I'd left."

"I would have found you. And I wouldn't have had to go looking. You'd have raced here on the first flight. Do you really think I don't understand? If you didn't come, you'd feel guilty if we killed somebody. And you don't like to feel guilty, isn't that right?"

Suddenly I realized that it was much easier to talk to this new unfamiliar Vadik. We now spoke as equals.

"Yes, that's right. No one goes looking for trouble. Okay, let's assume that we, Russians, fucked everybody over. Then who are you? An Eskimo?"

"I'm not Russian. I was Russian, but I don't want to be Russian any longer. Not-Russian—that's my nationality now. By the way, did your priest ask you to pass anything along to me?"

"No, he didn't. He only wanted to know about the rector, how he's doing. He said he didn't remember you."

"Really? He doesn't remember how he tried to break into my room when he got drunk at the Christmas party? He doesn't remember that? 'For God's sake, Vadik, open the door, help me relieve this burden, I love you . . . ' You know, he baptized me. I used to go to him for confessions . . . The rector is fine."

What the heck is going on? Is this some kind of truth and reconciliation day? And why do I need to know all this truth? What good is it? Although there had been rumors that Sasha was not only a skirt chaser but also had an eye for young men. I hadn't known about Vadik's conversion.

"Well, okay, I'm Russian, and you aren't. Don't you know how I felt about Chechnya? And what I think about Ukraine? But there's nothing I can do anymore."

"It's always like that with you—I didn't know, I didn't see, and I've always been against . . . And the result—another box in the cemetery. Lying, stealing, and killing—that's all you know how to do. Once in a hundred years, you send a Gagarin into space and feel so proud, it's as if you'd personally gone into space. Alexey Grigoriyevich used to tell me that when he was in the Gulag near Perm—Soviets convicted him as a nationalist—everyone tried to stick with their own people. Everyone but the Russians. They were like dogs . . . even dogs are better than you—they don't attack the weak."

"But what about Zhenya and me rescuing you? You and the three other guys? Doesn't that count for anything? And who took care of you later?"

"You? Us? You didn't give a shit about us. You wanted the glory. You were imagining how it would all look in the newspaper and on TV. You didn't even think of us as humans. I understood all that later, when I started to think back on things."

I didn't need to think back on it myself, because Vadik was right. Not completely, but for the most part. But how do you quantify these things—was it too much, too little? Was it all for nothing or did we do something right? Damn him!

Yes, we did care how it would look, on the page and on the screen, and how our colleagues would praise us for our exclusive. Of course, it was important to us, it was more important than anything in the world, why deny it now? But what could you expect? We were in our early twenties and suddenly, such good fortune came our way, something we couldn't have dreamed of—real, important, independent journalism. And there were no cooler journalists than us. And brilliant careers lay ahead of us in our chosen field, in our new country. Yes, you were material for us, but if we didn't give a shit about you, as you, Vadik, put it, you'd still be rotting in Chechnya. We could've put together a compassionate story about the prisoners, the innocent victims of fratricidal war, and left.

True, we didn't understand everything. That singer, Yuri Shevchuk, who was scorned by everyone back then for going to the garrisons to sing for the soldiers, he understood. He knew that these young men were fodder, the main victims in all this—and the main thing in general. And when it all started in Chechnya, Slava Izmailov, who'd been in Afghanistan, enlisted at his regional recruitment center and went to war along with the new recruits—he too understood. But the rest of us didn't. I didn't. It was easier for me to work with gangs of criminals—they were real victims, what else could they be? And it was easier to deal with them—you didn't need any accreditation. But Vadik, Sergey, and the two Olegs were just opportune cargo, although very useful, of course. It's easy to be a benefactor when you don't have to pay for it. And why not—we didn't turn a blind eye to the misfortunes of others.

"Let's finish this Dostoevskyian analysis. What's next?"

"What's next will be interesting. You love it when it gets interesting, don't you?"

"Love is not the right word."

"Well, you're about to get something interesting. Now, go to headquarters . . ."

Vadik wasn't asking anymore, and he wasn't proposing anything—he was giving orders.

A nd then they'll release all the hostages. No more conditions . . ."

They didn't look at me. They cast sidelong glances at one another, filled with fear and suspicion, having finally found out why we'd all gathered here today. Now they had to decide how to clean up this mess, and they were thinking about how much they didn't want to do that and about how cowardly they really were. Now, now, I thought vengefully, join us, now we're all in the same boat, one happy family, you can't jump off now.

"This will need to be reported, Viacheslav Igorevich . . ." the guy from the FSB said, addressing the foppish gentleman from the president's administration.

"Yes, it will," he agreed. "But as the head of the bureau, you, Valentin Nikolaevich, will need to report it. I'm here just as a consultant."

Valentin Nikolaevich responded to Viacheslav Igorevich with a glance that contained a great deal of sincere feeling— you slimy parasite, you rotten son of a bitch, as if I didn't know you were going to rush off and make a phone call . . . and I know who you'll be calling as well, and what you'll say; you don't need to tell me. I warned you, I told you that you needed to take preventative measures, so we didn't get into a situation like this, you used condom.

"I'll report to my superior. But I think it's wise to report it to the president."

After a short altercation, they arrived at the logical out-come: each would inform his superior, and as for the rest, let the higher ups decide. That's right, guys, let your superiors think about which one of you, to commemorate the success of the operation, will be sent to some Podunk town to run the fire department and which one will be sent to Sakhalin to oversee security at a fish factory.

Time for a cigarette break.

Sasha came over from somewhere off to the side and stood next to me.

"Give me a cigarette."

"But you don't smoke . . ."

"Who wouldn't smoke at a time like this? Well?"

"It's a military secret, sorry. But I have to be honest—it's gonna get worse for you. Isn't that right, Colonel?"

Semyonov was standing next to us. Incidentally, I was won-dering how you would describe his function: guarding a pro-tected person? He answered dully: "Yes."

"And Father Vladimir?"

"The rector? Vadik said he was okay, but I didn't see him for myself; they didn't let me in. By the way, Vadik remembers you, but you don't have to go there . . ."

Semyonov gave a warning cough.

"Okay, I'll be quiet."

I couldn't tell from Sasha's face if he was happy that he didn't have to do anything. Most likely, yes. Or was he happy that Vadik hadn't forgotten him. That was unlikely. It seems that Sasha had decided to show up on the scene because he felt that, sooner or later, they'd dig into that period of his life, and once they started digging, you never know what they might find. Better to get ahead of things. But why did he offer to take Zhenya's place? Did he know that Vadik would refuse? Or, in his newly discovered circumstances . . . ah, Father Alexander.

The door opened.

"Okay, that's it. They're calling me."

"Don't forget: Many are called but few are chosen."

"Thanks. I'm sorry."

"For what?"

"For thinking poorly of you."

Other than Tanya's ban on urination, this was probably the best thing I'd heard all day. This was my father's favorite quote, and Sasha knew it. Out of all my school friends who often hung out for days at our house, my father always singled out Sasha. I found out only later what they used to talk about and that it was my father who loaned Sasha a Bible to read. And now Sasha, who'd become an important figure in the Moscow Patriarchate, would drop in once a month, without fail, to see my father. One Easter, he even brought him a card from the Patriarch and laughed out loud as he told him how it killed the holy man to open the card in the same way he addressed the president: Dear Vladimir Vladimirovich.

Okay, let's get on with it, while we're still among the called. The trick is not to end up among the chosen. Or to get away in time.

There would be no announcements. We would ignore the terrorists' ultimatum and demand that they release the hostages immediately and surrender.

They call this front-page news?! Tanya had predicted it all the night before. But what would happen now?

Now it's time for the afterparty: "Approach them and propose a deal. If they release everyone and surrender, we can guarantee an eight-year sentence with the possibility of parole after four—provided none of the hostages is injured and there's no blood on their hands—and this would all quietly go away. We could even discuss charging them under a different article, not terrorism, but, say, malicious vandalism, which is six years maximum." "And if they ask, what guarantees?" "We have no interest in publicizing the matter, it's not in our interest to blow up the story. And, by the way, if it's a question of money, say, to support their family during their incarceration, tell them we're open to discussing any amount, any amount whatsoever."

Well, Vadik, I'm about to bring you the good news that you will soon be very rich . . .

A nd that's all they have to offer."

He didn't seem happy, sad, or surprised. Essentially, he had no reaction at all. He listened with complete indifference, as if it weren't his hide on the line.

"Okay. We have forty minutes left."

"Until what?"

"You'll find out. I need to ask you about something."

"Go ahead."

"If you had a newspaper, if your *Kuryer* was still publishing, or if you ran a television station, what would you do?"

"Today? Now?"

"No, I don't mean right now. Well, when everything really started in Ukraine, a year ago, or a year and a half . . ."

"I'm sorry, but that's a stupid question. That's exactly why I don't have either a newspaper or a television station. But why do you need to know this right now?"

"I just need to. Well? Why don't you have anything?"

"Well, when you've been put through the wringer . . . We tried to express all of our thoughts on the subject, and we were attacked from all sides."

"What, what did you try to say?"

"That it was madness what they were doing in Ukraine, that if Crimea was ours, then why were we stealing it? That we shouldn't start a war in Donbas for the sake of ratings, that it will all end in catastrophe."

"And?"

"What do you mean, and? You can see for yourself."

"But were you able to say all that before you got trampled?"

"I think so. Vadik, I don't understand what you want to hear."

"I want to understand why all your words missed the mark."

That was something I too wanted to understand. As Georgii Vladimirovich Strakhov used to say, if a story doesn't interest anyone, either the story itself is shit, or the writer is such as shithead that he could recite his multiplication tables, and no one would believe him.

"Okay, I'll answer you honestly. The problem is that, before, we had lied so much, withheld so much, and twisted the facts so much, that people stopped believing us."

"And did you lie too?"

"Maybe I didn't lie. Or twist the facts. But I didn't say anything to the people who did. I didn't stop shaking their hands, I continued to work with them. Some cursed them, but few criticized them out loud. And everyone lost their credibility as a result. Does that make sense?"

"Yes. Thanks. And so, no one will ever listen to you again?"

"We'll see. Some might, if we live long enough and exonerate ourselves. I wrote one story, exactly about this, but I won't trouble you . . ."

Vadik suddenly lost interest in our conversation. It was like a switch was turned off—his eyes closed, and he sat there, still and quiet . . . and then he came to.

"Well, they'll listen to you."

"Thank you very much for your high estimation of my perspective."

But Vadik wasn't listening to me anymore.

"It's time. The last parade is about to begin."

"What's happening?"

"It's time for you to go. Take all the people and leave."

"I don't understand."

"We'll need to organize the hostages now, then you'll take them out, but not all at once or they'll start a stampede. In groups of ten."

"And what about you? And the others?"

"We'll leave later."

"Without conditions? You don't have any demands?"

"Without conditions. We don't have any demands."

"I don't understand, Vadik . . ."

"You don't have to understand everything now. You will later."

I wasn't pleased. I was afraid. But of what? That I didn't understand Vadik's plan? Or was it the way he was speaking—slowly, pronouncing his words with difficulty . . .

"Should I go out and alert them?"

"You don't have to. They know."

"How?"

"They found out ten minutes ago."

Vadik took out his cell phone and showed me a message that had been posted ten minutes ago on the Internet. The author of that message was sitting in front of me.

"We seized the church and took hostages in the village of Nikolskoye. We summoned negotiators and told them our demands. We wanted the president of Russia to go on TV and apologize for two wars—the war in Chechnya and the one in Ukraine. He refused. We decided not to kill the hostages. We will release them. Although they are guilty. You are all guilty. And not just your president. You will be damned until you repent."

"Don't say anything, Uncle Pasha. The conversation is over. Say nothing and do what I told you."

The women came out first, in groups of ten, as Vadik had instructed. They all walked in the same way, with their heads down. Then the men came out, about thirty of them. I'd tried to keep track, but I had such a headache that I lost count. The priest, Father Vladimir, came out last.

Vladik stopped him in the doorway, holding onto the sleeves of his robe.

"We owe you some money. We took an advance but didn't have enough time to complete the work. I counted; we're returning thirty thousand rubles."

He pulled a wad of bills from an inside pocket and handed it to the rector, who stood there silently. He didn't put out his hand; his head was shaking almost imperceptibly.

"Take it. It'll come in handy."

Vadik shoved the money in the priest's hand and pushed him toward the doors. Father Vladimir took a step, then turned and blessed Vadik. It took him a while to open the door; he was pushing in the wrong direction. He was so nervous, he forgot which way the doors opened.

Vadik and I were the only two left.

"Vadik . . ."

"Everything's been said. The time for conversation is over."

"Then, good-bye."

"Why are you so sad? We might see each other again, right? We didn't kill anyone, we have no blood on our hands—we could make a deal. So, see you later."

"See you later, then."

Vadik suddenly smiled.

"That's completely different: see you later, see you later. It would be nice to see each other again. Say hi to everyone from me . . . promise me. And the main thing, don't forget why you came."

"What?"

A second later I was choking and wheezing because Vadik had grabbed me by the collar with both hands, pinned me to the wall and squeezed my throat so tightly that there were black circles floating before my eyes. He pronounced his words very distinctly and clearly, as if he were talking to a madman.

I did not walk out of the church, I flew. Vadik simply threw me out the doors and I barely remained on my feet. Behind me, the lock clicked in the iron-clad door. I caught my breath, spat, and walked away. I turned around once but saw only darkened windows; the spotlights had been turned off. And suddenly I understood what was going to happen, I understood very clearly . . . and so I tried to run or just to walk faster, but I felt I couldn't, I didn't have the strength and began to sway. I was fifty meters from the security outpost, and I could already make out Semyonov's silhouette. He was standing alone on the sidewalk. And I lumbered, like a cow toward a trough, with a heavy, steady gait.

The blast hit me before I heard the sound of the explosion.

I fell. I was blind. And deaf. I didn't see how the church collapsed then fell over the precipice.

When I came to and realized that I was alive and uninjured, I crawled on my hands and knees through the sticky spring mud, without looking back. I was just surprised that I could still think.

And why should I turn around? What do I want to see there? Do I have any desire to look at the wreckage of my former life? There will now be another life, a new one, without the Church of the Annunciation in Nikolskoye, without Vadik, a completely new life, but, most importantly, *not* without me, most importantly, I was alive. But I can't forget, I mustn't forget the important thing Vadik told me. I mustn't forget.

"Don't forget why you came. People will listen to you now. Settle the score." That's what Vadik said.

But settle up with whom? And for what? But most importantly, how?

He also said, "Forgive me." I also wanted to say, "Forgive me," but I didn't have time—he'd already closed the door.

# AFTERWORD
## BY LUDMILA ULITSKAYA

Journalistic prose is a distinct genre, but Mikhail Shevelev has transcended the limits of journalism and broken through into literature. Out of his reporting, as well as his in-depth and detailed knowledge of life in Russia during a difficult, agonizing, and ambiguous time, there emerges the profound story of a man, of his search for answers to the fundamental questions of existence, questions regarding one's personal responsibility for what is happening in the world, an individual's sense of self-worth, and notions of cruelty and mercy.

There is no wiseman in the world today who can explain the origin of individual and state terrorism, a pandemic of the twenty-first century. In the last century, the world lived through two psychic epidemics—communism and fascism—and millions of lives were lost on the battlefield and in concentration camps.

In the twenty-first century, terrorism is not based on a common ideology: the mass shooting of school children by a crazy teenager in the American heartland and the medieval execution of journalists by crazed soldiers of the Islamic State cannot be connected ideologically. But the spread of terrorism as a means of resolving personal or political problems is a sign of our times, a sign of the twenty-first century.

This book by Mikhail Shevelev does not pretend to offer a "general solution" to the problem. The job of an author is to address an individual case, the drama of an individual, but it is precisely through this individual case that the writer illuminates the psychological movements of the soul that compel that person to action. The author explores the fate of a young man, a soldier, a prisoner of war, a victim of social injustice and cruelty. He demands an answer from the head of state: For what purpose were the two Chechen wars unleashed? Why do the crimes committed by police go unpunished? Why has cruelty become a normal feature of human relationships? Shevelev's hero never gets an answer, but he calls off his act of terror, releasing the hostages from the church and blowing himself up along with his accomplices.

The hero commits a personal act of terror that is tantamount to an act of self-immolation, because he is held captive by one of the most seductive ideas there is—the idea of justice. But he does not find justice. There is no answer. Only one thing is constant: evil begets evil. A small act of evil begets a larger act, ad infinitum.

Look into your heart—don't we all bear responsibility for the bitterness and rage that surround us?

# GLOSSARY

Aushev, Ruslan (1954–) was president from 1993–2001 of the Republic of Ingushetia, within the Russian Federation, located in the North Caucasus. Before 2002, Nazran was the capital of Ingushetia; then it moved to Magas.

Basayev, Shamil (1965–2006) was a leader of the Chechen independence movement and a guerrilla commander. He is believed to have been the mastermind behind the Budyonovsk Hospital raid in 1995, the Beslan school siege in 2004, the attack on the Dubrovka Theater in 2002, and the Russian aircraft bombings in 2004. He died in 2006 in an accident during an arms deal.

Chernomyrdin, Viktor (1938–2010) was the prime minister of Russia (1992–1998) under Boris Yeltsyn's presidency and was and the first chairman of the Gazprom energy company.

Chirikova, Yevgeniya (1976–) is a Russian environmental activist, known mostly for her campaigns to preserve the forests along a new highway connecting Moscow and St. Petersburg and near the city of Khimki, near Moscow. She took part in the protests of 2011–2013 that followed the disputed parliamentary elections in 2011.

Dr. Liza (Elizaveta Glinka) (1962–2016) was a Russian charity activist and humanitarian. Recognized by the Russian government for her charitable work, she died in the 2016 Russian Defense Ministry Tupolev Tu-154 crash.

FSB is the abbreviation for the Russian Federal Security Service, or *Federal'naia Sluzhba Bezopasnosti*, the main successor agency of the Soviet KGB and the principal agency for maintaining domestic security.

GKChP is the abbreviation for the State Committee on the State of Emergency, or *Gosudarstvennyi Komitet po chrezvychainomu polozheniiu*, made up of eight high-ranking Soviet officials from the government, the Communist Party and the KGB who attempted to oust Mikhail Gorbachev in a coup d'état on August 19, 1991. The coup failed and the provisional government collapsed just days later, on August 22.

Gusinsky, Vladimir (1952–) is a Russian media tycoon. He founded the Media-Most holding company, which included NTV free-to-air channel, the newspaper *Segodnya*, the radio station Ekho Moskvy, and a number of magazines. In May 2000, Putin authorized an investigation against Gusinsky in an attempt to place NTV under government control and silence the opposition. Gusinsky left Russa in 2015.

Khamatova, Chulpan (1975–) is a Russian actress and philanthropist. She supported Putin in the 2012 election, supposedly to save her children's charity. Following the outbreak of the Russian war in Ukraine, she chose to remain in Latvia where she was vacationing.

Khodorkovsky, Mikhail (1963–) is an exiled Russian businessman, now residing in London. From 1997–2004, he was the first chairman and CEO of Yukos Oil and was at the time believed to be the richest man in Russia. An increasingly vocal critic of Putin, he was arrested in 2003 on corruption charges and served almost eight years in prison.

Kiselyov, Yevgeny (1956–) is a Russian television journalist. He was the host of a popular weekly news show on NTV in the 1990s, which criticized government corruption and Boris Yeltsyn.

Latynina, Yulia (1966-) is a Russian writer and journalist. She is a columnist for the newspaper *Novaya Gazeta* and the most popular host at the Ekho Moskvy radio station. Latynina has written more than twenty books, including fantasy and crime fiction. She is the author of *The Insider* and *Not Human*. A strong opponent of Putin, she left Russia in 2017.

Maskhadov, Aslan (1951–2005) was a Soviet and Chechen politician. He was the third president of the Chechen Republic of Ichkeria, which has never been officially recognized.

Masyuk, Yelena (1966–) is a Russian television journalist known for her coverage of the Chechen Wars.

MChS is the abbreviation for the Russian Ministry of Emergency Situations, or *Ministerstvo Chrezvychainykh Situatsii*, a Russian federal ministry that oversees the government response to natural disasters and terrorist attacks. It is known internationally as EMERCOM, derived from Emergency Control Ministry.

Mikhailov, Aleksandr (1951–2020) was a Russian politician, a member of the State Duma, and the governor of Kursk Oblast. He was a member of the Communist Party until 2004 and then switched his affiliation to the United Russia party, led by Vladimir Putin. He was embroiled in controversy in 2010 over antisemitic remarks.

MVD is the abbreviation for the Russian Ministry for Internal Affairs, or *Ministerstvo Vnutrennykh Del,* which is responsible for law enforcement. Its agencies include the Police of Russia, Migration Affairs, Drugs Control, Traffic Safety, and the Center for Combating Extremism.

Navalny, Alexei (1976–) is a Russian lawyer, anti-corruption activist, and an opposition leader. He was convicted of embezzlement in 2014 and was barred from running in the 2018 presidential election. In August of 2020 he was poisoned by the Soviet nerve agent Novochuk, for which he accused the Putin government. He was allowed to go to Germany for treatment but was then arrested on his return to Russia for violating his parole and sentenced to two and a half years in prison. He is recognized by Amnesty International as a prisoner of conscience, and in 2021 he was awarded the Sakharov Prize for his human rights work.

Politkovskaya, Anna (1958–2006) was a Russian journalist and human rights activist known for her reports on political events in Russia, especially during the Second Chechen War. She was murdered in the elevator in her apartment building. The five men who carried out the murder were convicted and sent to prison, but it is still unclear who ordered and paid for the killing.

Razgon, Lev (1908–1999) was a Soviet journalist, writer, and human rights activist. He spent almost ten years in the

Gulag, first from 1938–1942, and then from 1950–1955. In 1988, his Gulag memoir *True Stories* was released: that same year he left the Communist Party.

Shevchuk, Yuri (1957–) is a Soviet and Russian rock musician. He is a singer-songwriter and a leader of the rock group DDT. During the First Chechen War, Shevchuk went to Chechnya and gave fifty concerts for Russian troops and Chechen citizens alike. He is a strong opponent of Putin. On 24 February 2022, after the Russian invasion of Ukraine, Shevchuk stated: "Our future is being taken from us. We're being pulled as if through an ice hole into the past, into the 19th, 18th, 17th century. And people refuse to accept it."

Sobchak, Ksenia (1981–) is a socialite, television personality, and a journalist. She holds dual, Russian-Israeli, citizenship. She is the daughter of Russian senator Lyudmila Narusova and Anatoly Sobchak, the first democratically elected mayor of St. Petersburg and mentor to Vladimir Putin and Dmitry Medvedev.

Stepashin, Sergei (1952–) is a Russian politician. He served briefly as the prime minister of Russia in 1999. He was the head of the Federal Security Service at the time of the terrorist attack on the Budyonovsk hospital; he resigned after the failed rescue attempt.

Strugatsky Brothers is a reference to Arkady and Boris Strugatsky, who were enormously popular authors of science fiction in the post-war Soviet Union. They collaborated throughout most of their careers. Many of their novels, such as *Roadside Picnic* and *Hard to Be a God*, were interpreted in late Soviet culture as works of social criticism.

TASS is the abbreviation for the state-owned Russian news agency Telegraph Agency of Communication and Messages (*Telegrafnoye Agentstvo Svazi i Soobshcheniya*), founded in 1904. Before 1992, the acronym stood for *Telegrafnoye Agentstvo Sovetskogo Soyuza,* or the Telegraph Agency of the Soviet Union.